DRESSING UP STELLA

KIM SMART

Thanks to my family and friends who continue to encourage me to follow my dreams. This one's for you!

CONTENTS

Chapter 1	1
Chapter 2	11
Chapter 3	21
Chapter 4	32
Chapter 5	42
Chapter 6	54
Chapter 7	67
Chapter 8	77
Chapter 9	89
Chapter 10	101
Chapter 11	113
Chapter 12	124
Chapter 13	137
Chapter 14	147
Chapter 15	160
Chapter 16	173
Chapter 17	187
Chapter 18	201
Chapter 19	210
Acknowledgments	217
About the Author	219
Also by Kim Smart	221

1

———————

Clara Drake was half of the duo that managed a collection of ranches in Arizona, including their home place where Stella Davies worked as a cowboy. She welcomed Stella into their home, showed her to the sitting room and poured them each a cup of coffee.

"Thanks for coming in Stella." Clara's voice was pensive. "I was sitting here thinking about the day you showed up here and won our hearts. You were a young woman on a mission to prove you could handle yourself, the men around you, cattle and horses. You had twice the grit of any of our hands and ambition driving you like a steam engine!"

"Oh, that was an interesting time. I remember. I was dumped in New Mexico by a guy, some wildcat who did something, I'll never know what, to get run off that ranch. Hank. He sure wooed me, a naive young girl from a small South Dakota ranch who was far too trusting." Stella placed her hand on Clara's and looked into her kind eyes. "I'm so grateful they took me in when Hank abandoned me and recommended I come here with you and Martin. You have been such a godsend for me."

Stella meant every word. She loved working for the Drakes and felt right at home with the rest of the crew, all men.

"And you for us. You impressed us with your grit. More than that, your skills make you a standout amongst all our crew. Martin will be here soon. We want to discuss a proposal with you. But he had to take a call. While we have some time, though, I wonder Stella, do you ever think of having a family? I'm not asking as your boss. I'm asking as a fellow woman. I remember the early days when Martin and I were first starting our business. We couldn't afford many hired hands, so I did a lot of the trail work with him. I rode throughout my pregnancy but when our baby was born he was so sick that I had to stay home with him. Oh, my, now that sounds so morbid. I guess my message to you is that you can have it all. You can have your work and a family."

"Thank you, Clara. That's something my mom says too. I'm sorry you had such a limited time with your son. You both talk so fondly about him, it's apparent you loved him and were wonderful parents." Stella looked to the picture on the fireplace mantle: new parents holding a sweet baby boy in a baptismal gown. Clara and Martin's only child had fatal heart defects that took his life as a toddler. Photos and mementos were scattered throughout the house and they shared their story with anyone who would listen.

"I have thought little about it. I came from a great family. I have three super brothers and it would be natural to think I would want a family. Right now I'm so in love with my work and enjoy working outside. My heart is full. I never thought of courting any of my male co-workers. I might feel differently if a suitor swept me off my feet. I don't get off the ranch much. I go to town to the feed and tack store or such. There is little chance of me meeting someone. I'm fine with that right now." Clara nodded in understanding as Stella spoke.

"Good morning, Stella! My apologies for keeping you waiting." Martin joined them in the sitting room. Stella's stomach swirled as he reached out his hand. She wasn't nervous about this meeting here, the business center of a huge operation, until this moment. She stood and shook his hand.

"Oh, it's no problem. I got up early to get a jump-start on my chores." Stella needed to assure them she was on top of her work. It was important for her to be a stellar worker.

"Of course you did." Martin grinned widely at Stella. His whole friendly face lit up, distracting from the weathered lines from decades of working in the desert of Arizona.

"Stella, we called you here today to talk about an opportunity that would be a promotion for you. We believe you're up for it, but we will lay it out for you and you must decide if this is the right thing for you, or not. There is a lot to consider and there will be new things for you to learn."

"Well, you've piqued my interest."

"Okay. Let's talk. One of our holdings is a ranch further north. You've probably heard us talk about it before and honestly, I don't remember, you may have visited it. It's Rabbit Creek Ranch, northwest of here, about eighty miles."

"I dropped a load of salt up there two, maybe three years ago. It seemed like a quiet part of the country. More rugged than here."

"You're right. It is more rugged and the temperatures are more extreme. The winter is harsher up there than it is here, even though we are not so far apart. We've had a good fella up there running cattle for us, but he's ready to retire. Well, his wife is ready for him to retire. She has some health problems and needs him to be around home more."

"Oh, I'm sorry to hear that. If I recall, his name is Jed. Jed O'Reilly."

"That's right. See Clara, I told you she had a mind like a steel trap."

"You did, and she does." Clara smiled at them both.

"Life's different for the foreman up there. We don't have permanent housing since the cattle run on BLM land under a long-term lease. The pay is enough for you to pick up a modest home in Watson or a nearby town. If you need help with a down payment, we could work something out there, too. But here's the thing you should know about. It's a different model of ranching than the rest of our operation. You have to move the cattle more frequently. It's required as part of our agreement with the feds when we lease the land. When you move them, you stay out in the elements with them, year-round."

"That sounds interesting. How long has Jed been up there doing this work for you?"

"Well, we looked that up the other day. Seems he's been there for fourteen years. He worked for another rancher with a similar set-up, but somehow…" Martin looked at Clara and winked. "We enticed him to come work for us. He's been happy with us. I'm sure he would chat with you and he agreed to show whoever comes on board around the place. There are millions of acres of land up there and he's worked out a rotation schedule that seems reasonable. It is something you should review, along with maximizing the cow-calf pairs the land will support. We can't over-graze but need to use what's available to us under the lease."

"Sure, that makes sense. I've heard of these lease arrangements before. As I recall, the cow-calf annual grazing fee is reasonable for the rancher."

"That's right, it is, and all the more reason for us to maximize the grazing by careful rotations where we can." Martin loved the cattle business and made it a point to be familiar with the big players across the country. His was a unique operation, but he loved learning from others. He was always looking for the best practice in animal health. He wanted the most natural environment possible for his herds. Market demands for such things as soy-free and grass-fed cattle without hormones were near and dear to him. The health of their herds was vitally important.

"So, can you tell me more about the days or weeks, what they look like? Is there fencing to maintain and sorting pens and such?"

"Great questions. The weeks look different. Some weeks you will deliver minerals and salt to the pastures. At other times you will sleep under the stars and drive cattle from one pasture to the next. It's a different breed of cattle and they are darn smart. The older cows, we have a few of them, are familiar with the rotation. Once they get headed in the right direction, they lead the others right down the path. It's the darnedest thing I ever saw."

"That's amazing. I saw that growing up but our cattle rotated between two huge pastures, not several."

"Well, the other thing that's interesting there is the terrain. It's rugged with steep gorges covered in rock, cactus, and brush. You must test your horses out there to see if they're up to it. It takes a confident, sure-footed horse to negotiate that land. We have wall tents and small storage sheds set up in strategic places. Cooking over a campfire is a way of life. There are a half-dozen hands Jed has worked with. None of them work full time for Rabbit Creek. They can help with cattle drives and big projects. He used some hands to patch a long line of fence and do some other repairs that he couldn't do himself in a day or so." Martin paused, trying to measure Stella's reaction.

"It takes someone who enjoys being alone. I've watched you around here. You're good around people but, unlike some folk, you don't seem to need to be talking or going to town to party on your days off. Maybe I got that wrong, and you must let me know, but Clara and I have discussed this and wanted to give you the first opportunity at the job."

"I am honored that you would pick me. I am very much interested and, to be sure I've got the full picture and haven't romanticized it too much, could I meet with Jed for a day and have him show me around?"

"Yes, yes! Jed's in the middle of a move right now so I can't just send you up. You'll never find him. But when he gets back from that, I'll set up a day for you to go up there and chat with him. It may be a good time to look around for housing too. The nearest is about thirty miles from the entrance to the BLM property.

That way you could get a feel for what's in the area."

"From a safety perspective, we provide a satellite phone. Cellular phones don't work so well up there. It's too far between towers." Clara wanted Stella to be assured that communication would be available, even if she found herself alone in the canyon.

"Also, for safety, you'll know that there, like around here, there are snakes and coyotes and bobcats and such. We've never had a problem with attacks on humans. We lost two or three calves in all the years we've been up there. Honestly, I don't think that's too bad." Martin could look in his books and know for certain if need be. He kept meticulous notes on his cattle.

"No, that's not bad at all. I mean, you hate losing any and feel just awful for those little guys, but when you're tangling in nature, it happens." Stella thought back to a time on Buffalo Ridge Ranch when a pack of wolves passed through and took down three calves before the activity in the field caught the family's attention. The whole family grieved the losses.

"Well, Clara said she wanted to take you to the kitchen and get your help with a project in there. I've got another meeting with a young fella, Brandon Cage. You ever heard of him?"

"No, I haven't heard that name."

"Well, he's an up-and-coming lawyer for the cattleman. He's coming out here to chat with me about the future of ranching. Brandon wants to bend my ear a bit and then have me give him some secrets. I've known the family for a long time. Good people. If our meeting gets done, I'd like you to meet him. I think you're about the same age."

"Sounds good." Stella shook Martin's hand. She looked at Martin, then Clara. "Thank you both for this opportunity. I'm ninety percent certain it's right for me and can let you know for sure after I've spent a little time with Jed."

"That is perfect. We want you to be aware of what you're getting into. Well, I see Brandon's pickup pulling in. I'll let you two head off to do whatever it is Clara has in mind and talk to you later."

2

Martin greeted Brandon in the yard, as he got out of his pickup. "Brandon! Sure is good to see you, young man."

"You too Martin, and before I forget, my parents send all their best to you and Clara. In fact…" Brandon reached through the open window of the pickup and pulled out a paper bag with handles. "Mom sent this lemon blueberry Bundt cake."

"Well now, Sandy is always doing something nice for someone. I'm glad to be on the receiving end today. Let's you and I walk this to the kitchen. Clara's back there with one of the cowboys looking at something. I'd like to introduce you to her."

"Her?" Brandon knew a lot of women who

worked on ranches with their husbands but never heard one referred to on a working ranch like Martin's as a cowboy.

"That's right. Stella's the most talented cowboy I've got. She's been with us, oh, I'd say about four years now, and can outride any man around. Smart, too. I met with her this morning and mentioned that I'd like to introduce the two of you. Anyway, you're both good folk and both love cattle so, there ya go."

The men walked down the long hallway from the front door to the interior courtyard and then into the kitchen where Clara and Stella sat at the kitchen table looking over some old recipe books.

"Well, if it isn't little Brandon Cage!" Clara hopped up from her chair and threw her arms around Brandon for a big western welcome. "I guess I'll have to drop the little, won't I?"

"Yes, ma'am. I'm afraid I've grown up."

"And a lawyer now, to boot. How are your folks?"

"Well, they are great Clara. Here…" Brandon held out the paper bag. "Mom sent this cake along for you."

"Isn't she the sweetest? Brandon, this is my friend, Stella Davies. Stella is our best hand and, being she's also a woman raised on a ranch with a mess of boys in the family, I pulled her in here to give me some ideas for recipes. Sometimes I bore myself making and serving the same old things over and over again."

Brandon held his hand out for Stella. She took it, surprised at the strength and roughness of his hands, something she didn't expect from a lawyer. "It's a pleasure to meet you, Brandon." She smiled confidently, as if she was in a business meeting. Yet she couldn't help but notice the steel-blue eyes against the tanned skin and three-day stubble on his square jaw… far more handsome than any man she'd worked with in the last several years.

Brandon shook her hand and held it a little longer than one would expect. Stella mesmerized him. She was raw beauty with thick dark hair pulled back into a long braid down her back, dark pools for eyes, and flawless skin kissed by the sun.

"And you as well, Stella."

Martin and Clara looked at each other and smiled, a sparkle in their eyes. They had played matchmaker a time or two before and didn't profess to be experts, but when the potential for this introduction arose they knew they just had to make it happen. They loved them both as if they were their own children.

"Well, son, I think we have some business to talk about." Martin put his arm around Brandon's shoulder and ushered him back through the courtyard to the office. Their conversation trailed off as they moved away from the kitchen.

"Brandon's folks have been at this business out here about as long as we have. Brandon is their youngest. He's got two older sisters and an older brother. We've watched them all grow up. A bunch of fine young folks who are all set out to improve the world. Love them all." Clara smiled as she talked about the Cage family. It reminded Stella of her own family and the close family friends she grew up with.

"He seems like a nice guy."

"Good looking, too, don't you think?"

"Clara! What would Martin say?" The two laughed as they sat back down to look over the recipe books. They picked out four new recipes for Clara to test. Stella told Clara about her mother's famous lasagna, something Stella could not remember eating here at the Winding Slough Ranch.

"Lasagna. I've never made it. I thought it always looked so darn complicated that I never even tried."

"Not at all. Tell you what, if you need some help, I'll be glad to help. Let me write down the recipe for you. Mom combines several recipes, and it's the best."

Clara clapped her hands. "Well, that would be terrific! I have to say, it's so nice to have another woman to chat with. But I've taken you away from your work long enough. I'm sure you'd rather be outside with the herd. I thank you for spending some time with me."

"Oh, it's my pleasure. I'm not opposed to being domestic. I like that, too. It reminds me of spending time in the kitchen with my mom."

"Isn't it about time you pay your folks a visit?" Clara often encouraged Stella to take some time off and see her family. She had gone back to South Dakota only once in the years she worked for them.

"I thought about that. Maybe, if this promotion works out for me, I can take a few days before the transition and go home to see them. Will Jed and his wife be okay with that?"

"They would. His wife's condition is ongoing and while it's getting worse over time, she's not in critical condition just yet."

"I hope it works out."

Clara escorted Stella to the front of the house, passing the office. The door was ajar and the women could hear the men talking, catching familiar words like market share and feed sources.

"I've been out canvassing ranchers, trying to get a feel for the issues they face. But on the other side, I'm also listening to consumer groups and getting a feel for what they are searching for when they go to the stores. Not everyone is turning to veganism like the media once led us to believe." Brandon focused on agriculture when he was in law school and interned with a large agricultural lobby firm. He learned a lot, but lobbying was too far from the ranch for him. He wants to be closer to the food source and never leave behind his ranching roots.

"Well, I said it when the talking heads were trying to convince us all ten years ago that cattle were ruining the environment and causing climate change. They claimed that…" Martin motioned with air quotes. "Research shows nobody will eat beef. As we've seen, there are many advocates for clean beef as a modality to heal the body. Just last week I was listening to one of those videos online where a health expert was showing, using science, how clean beef, in their terms 'grass-fed, soy and hormone-free beef', healed cells badly damaged by stress."

Martin enjoyed staying current with health trends and finding information that supported the clean ranching methods he preferred. "As you know, my cattle are grass-fed and grass-finished. They never see a lick of feed, soy or otherwise, and I wouldn't dare give these cows hormones. They are perfect just the way they are, especially those up north that navigate that difficult terrain."

"What's that you have up north, Martin? You running something different up there than you are here?"

"That's right. I run all Barzona up there, on BLM land."

"No kidding! I didn't realize you had that operation up there, besides these other ranches you're operating."

"It's a great deal and honestly, with me they have a responsible tenant. I don't know if, across the country where they have these programs, they have the same experience but I want this program to be a great success. My lease is cheap but I keep up all the fences, watch the land, graze responsibly to reduce fire risk and such and pay my taxes when I sell the cattle. That young woman you just met, I'm thinking of sending her up there to run the operation. The guy I have had in place for several years needs to retire for family reasons."

"Stella, right?"

"Yeah. Stella Davies. Comes from a ranching family in the Badlands of South Dakota. Quite a story how she got here, but I'll leave that for her to tell. Anyway, she rides circles around some of these fellas I got working here. She's got more ambition in her pinky than most grown men have altogether."

"I suppose it's not proper for me to ask, but could I have her number? She seems like someone I should get to know and, wow, what a beauty she is. Does she date anyone or is she not inclined to date men?"

"Stella is a workhorse and a professional. She wouldn't consider dating a co-worker. Wouldn't want there to be any conflict and honestly, she doesn't go to town much except for the essentials. Honing her skills and practicing her craft has been Stella's focus in her time with us. She's an amazing young woman. None of these other cowboys can throw a rope like she can. Stella's got a brother on the professional bull riding circuit. Chance Davies. Maybe you've heard of him."

"To tell you the truth, I have had little time to follow the rodeo scene. I will look him up. Now, about that number, do you think she would mind if you gave it to me?"

"Brandon, I have so much respect for her

that I must ask her. If she says it's okay, I'll gladly give it to you. We think the world of both of you and hey, if a chance meeting here at our place sparks an interest, it would warm our hearts."

The men continued their conversation, testing the climate change arguments, opining on animal health, food safety, international import impacts to the U.S. market, pricing strategies, consumer demands and beef processing regulations. They didn't solve any problems, but enjoyed a robust exchange of ideas. They agreed to resume their conversation in two months and to continue to do so as long as the dialogue remained interesting and fruitful.

"Well, I've got to head back to Phoenix."

"Say, how are those boys treating you there at the firm?"

"Not too bad. I'm the new kid on the block, and I'm very much in learning mode. They give me all kinds of opportunities for new experiences, and there are great mentors. I'm there for the experience. It's not what I ultimately desire to do. I'm more interested in working at the grassroots level, not the corporate level. The law firm is geared toward the latter, but I will undoubtedly gain great experience from talented attorneys."

"That's good to hear. Do you get much opportunity to see the folks at the ranch?"

"I try to get out there every weekend if possible, and on holidays. It's in my blood and I need my fix more than I need to be in the city going to the clubs. I did a bit of that in college and quickly learned it wasn't for me."

"That's what I figured. I think your brother and sisters were like that, too. Salt of the earth people, all of you."

"Well, we had the best teachers, and they had the best friends, like you and Clara."

"Son, it's been great chatting with you, and I promise I'll check in with Stella and send you an answer just as soon as I have it."

"Thank you, Martin. I look forward to our next meeting and I'll get some of that research together that we discussed."

"Fantastic. I look forward to it too." Martin was excited to be engaged on the front end of Brandon's career. He wanted the opportunity to provide Brandon with insights into what he saw as the most pressing issues, both now and in the future.

3

The second Saturday after her chance encounter with Brandon Cage, Stella's phone rang. It was Brandon, inviting her out for dinner.

"How do you feel about authentic Mexican food? There's a great place in town. It's just a hole in the wall, not much seating but the food is wonderful." Brandon knew the family well and could reserve a table for two, despite the no-reservations policy.

Stella hesitated at first, only because she liked her solitude and looked forward to her weekends to relax and clean tack and do other things she couldn't get to during the busy week. "That sounds good for a change."

"Great. I'll pick you up next Saturday, say about seven?"

"I'll be ready and waiting." Stella contemplated countering and meeting him in town. She preferred to be as casual as possible. With a promotion hanging in the wings, a relationship wasn't on her agenda just now. However, she took him up on his offer because anything she picked up in town would have to sit in her pickup until after dinner, and that could be a disaster.

Stella casually told Clara about the date. She would see Brandon's pickup anyway, so she might as well let her know.

Clara played down her inner enthusiasm. "Well, isn't that nice dear? I hope you two have a wonderful time. Where did you say you were going for dinner?"

"Casa de Francisco, he called it. Are you familiar with the restaurant?"

"Sure, I am. They've been in business for eons and we've been many times. Their food has never disappointed me. Last time I was there, I had the carne asada. Nobody makes it better."

"You can tell me then. It's casual, right? I mean it wouldn't be good to overdress."

"It is casual. Besides, you look great in whatever you wear, dirty dungarees after branding included."

"You're so sweet, Clara. I own a dress or at least a skirt so I could dress up, but my rhinestone jeans are about as fancy as I prefer to be."

"Well dear, those will be just fine."

"Thank you, Clara. I've got to get back to work. Just wanted you to know when you saw Brandon's pickup in the yard why he was here."

"Thanks. I will let Martin know too." Clara opened the door for Stella to leave, almost rushing her out. She stood at the screen door a moment and waved Stella off before hustling to Martin's office. "Wouldn't ya know? Brandon Cage is taking Stella out on a date."

"Of course he is." Martin looked up from his desk and over his reading glasses.

"What do you mean, of course he is?" Clara could tell by the grin curling at the edges of Martin's mouth that he had a hand in this new development.

"Martin, what did you do?"

"Well, last time Brandon was out here visiting, he asked for her number. I told him I would have to clear it with Stella first and, I did. So…" Martin looked at his calendar. "It took Brandon exactly three days to make that call."

"Guess he's wasting no time and he

shouldn't. She's a catch." Clara had grown to love Stella like the daughter she never had and wanted the greatest happiness for her.

———

The week was busy for Stella, as they all seemed to be. On Wednesday she drove up north and met with Jed, the foreman at Rabbit Creek Ranch. She spent the entire day looking at maps, herd records, weather histories and siphoning every bit of useful information she could from Jed.

"You have been wonderful to share all this information and your tremendous knowledge, Jed. I have just two questions left for you, is that all right?"

"Sure, Stella. Shoot." Jed poured the last bit of coffee from the thermos into his cup after Stella waved him away from her cup. She was wired enough by the experience; she didn't need more caffeine.

"Okay. So the first one is, what is the hardest part of this job? I mean, it's unique from what most cowboys do and I'm not sure I can anticipate every challenge that may come up."

"That's right, you can't. But what you've been doing is a good background for this kind of work. For me, two things have been challenging. First, the uncertainty of predators out here, more for the cattle than for me. Fortunately, we lost only a couple head since I've been here, but every time I head up the trail I fret that I might find mayhem at the other end. Maybe that's just me, I'm a worrier."

"Oh, that makes perfect sense to me and I've thought a lot about it already. I would feel so responsible if something happened to the herd."

"That's the thing. The owners and the government all know the risks so if something happens, I'm telling you now, you can't take it personally."

"I hear you. I hope I don't have to practice your advice much."

"Me too, for your sake. It will take a toll on ya if you let it."

"You said there were two things. What's the second?"

"Well, the second is particular to my circumstances and you shouldn't bother yourself none with it. This job was working fine for the wife and me. She didn't mind being home, spending more time with our kids and then our grandkids, but now that she's got the cancer she needs me home and, bless her heart, she wants me there, too."

"I'm so sorry those are the circumstances you landed in Jed. I wish you and your wife the best life you can have under the circumstances. It can't be easy."

"No, it's not. But then, nothing about our life has been easy and nobody said it would be so we're doing just fine. I think you had a second question for me."

"Oh, yeah, that's right. You've only just met me and know little about me, but based on your experience and what little you do know, what do you see as the hardest part of the job for me?"

"Oh, that's easy. I mean nothing crude by this ma'am, but you're a pretty gal and not all the guys that come to work with you are going to take you seriously if you know what I mean. You may spend more time fending them off than herding the cattle when you're working. I would just say to you, pick your hands carefully. Make it clear from the get-go that you're the boss and there's no messing with you. You may even need to make up a story about having a husband or something just for an extra buffer."

"Well now, that's interesting. I've been fortunate so far. There's been a couple of fellas that thought they had a chance, but I quickly turned that around. I'll keep your advice in mind and appreciate you bringing it to my attention, Jed."

"You bet, ma'am. Now, if there's nothing else today, I've a need to get home. You have my number. Call me any old time you need something. Honestly, I won't mind and will welcome the opportunity to hear about the operation."

"That's very kind of you. I will take you up on that offer. Thank you." Stella shook Jed's hand and crawled into her pickup, satisfied with what she had learned throughout the day. She wanted the promotion - isolation, risky hands and all.

Stella stopped to look at three homes for sale in a nearby community before she headed back. She wanted something small, but with pasture and protection for her horses. An outbuilding to store her four-wheeler and horse trailer would be a nice perk. Stella wanted to do something besides spend time at home cleaning, so the smaller the house the better.

The places she saw were equally suitable, and their prices were consistent with the amenities they offered. When the time came, she was certain she could find her next home without difficulty. After hearing the exact terms of the promotion, she would need to review her finances carefully. All things considered, she was ready to deliver her final decision to Martin and Clara. Stella wanted to make the move.

As she drove to the ranch, Stella remembered the upcoming date with Brandon. *"Dang!"* she thought. *"Why did I say yes?"*

She was happy without the interference of a man taking her away from the world she lived in and loved. She was not eager to complicate her life.

"Those eyes, that handsome face!" She realized why she agreed to go out. Between his good looks and her mother's regular encouragement to "just test the waters", she struck an opportunity that rarely presented itself in her small world.

As the miles passed, Stella ran through her wardrobe options. They were limited. Even her good boots had taken some rides and were showing their wear. Her sneakers would be too casual and flip-flops, well, they never left her bunkhouse.

Stella's one pair of dress jeans sparkled with rhinestones that accented her toned backside. She hadn't worn them in over a year, but they would fit. Stella was always told that the most flattering colors for her were turquoise, berry, red and forest green. Red was not an option for this date and she was never fond of forest green, finding it too drab and causing her to look pale. She used to have a nice cotton berry-colored dress shirt, but over the years it became a work shirt. That left one turquoise western shirt. It had long sleeves, but for an evening dinner it would work okay.

If she had a second date with Brandon or anyone, a dreaded shopping trip would be in order. Maybe if she mentioned it to her mother, Yvette would shop for her. *"Should I give these details to Mom? Give her an inch and she'll take a mile. Next thing I know, she'll be planning a wedding simply because I had one date."*

No. Stella would do her own shopping, even if it were online. But no need to get ahead here, the first date had not yet happened. Stella had never even told her mother about Hank, the good-looking cowboy who lured her away from South Dakota right out of high school. Her parents thought she was off giving riding lessons at an elite training center. Stella was too embarrassed to let them know that a no-good, lying cowboy dumped her on a ranch in New Mexico. The owners threw him off the ranch, leaving Stella somewhere northwest of Santa Fe, over eight hundred miles from Buffalo Ridge Ranch and the protective arms of her parents.

Something in Stella took hold when Hank abandoned her. Reaching as deep as she could, she mustered the grit to hold her head high and not feel defeated. Stella escaped what could have been a very difficult relationship and an unsafe lifestyle, with no promise of anything except adventure, not all of which would have been in her best interest.

She felt many times that she had guardians with her, silently encouraging her to drive for her dreams. That forced her to decide early on what it was she wanted to be. Stella would continue in the Davies tradition and be the best cowboy she could be. She had already done well as an amateur barrel racer, but she wasn't looking for glory or the showy glamour of a rodeo queen. She wanted dust on her boots, grime in her ears and dried leaves in her hair after a hard day's work in the open air. Stella got that most days and most days were exceedingly happy.

By the time Stella got back to her bunkhouse, dusk had arrived and it was time to settle in for the night. She checked her horses, sent Martin a text requesting a meeting to discuss the Rabbit Creek Ranch opportunity. She didn't expect to hear from him until morning, but before she lay her head down for the night, Martin responded and set an appointment for Saturday morning.

Just three days. She would have to try hard to keep her mind on her work. Already she was visualizing herself sleeping in open grazing land and setting up her own house. She thought about inviting her mother out, once she found a house, to domesticate her new abode. Shopping for matching shower curtains and towels was not Stella's forte, and she knew it. If she tried, Stella could pick out the living room and bedroom furniture, but she had never had to test those skills. It would be a new adventure in many ways. Two new adventures converging at once was almost overwhelming for Stella. She lay in bed counting cattle in her mind's eye until she fell asleep.

4

"Well Stella, here we are again. And just look at you! I don't know if I've ever seen you so dressed up for a meeting."

Stella had showered and put her dress clothes on. She had polished up a pair of leather ankle boots she found in the back of her meager shoe collection.

"Yeah, well, I'll be heading out to dinner later and only wanted to dress once today. You know me, always looking for efficiencies."

It was late afternoon. Martin had scheduled the meeting to occur just before Brandon arrived. He felt somewhat responsible and a little fatherly toward Stella. He wanted to be sure Brandon knew he and Clara were looking out for Stella's best interest. Not exactly like a father with a shotgun sitting on the porch waiting for his daughter to return from a date, but almost.

"You drove up to Rabbit Creek and met with Jed. How did that go?"

"Jed was very open. He showed me around, gave me mounds of information and answered all my questions. He even gave me his cell number so I could contact him if I had questions. I have to say, he also gave me some sage advice, and that was well worth the trip."

"That Jed has been a good hand. He's old school so if you take this job, know that Clara and I are open to discuss any suggestions for changes and improvements you may come up with. Don't get me wrong; I have no complaints about how the operation has been doing. I am mindful that we must always adjust and improve with changing times."

"Yes, that's right, and you modeled that here for me in the years I've been working with you. I'm grateful for the open door for discussions and, yes, I am interested in the position after meeting with Jed. I would like to hear about the compensation package. I took a little time Wednesday to look at properties around Watson. I wanted to scope the area to see what's available but, as you said before, this would differ from what I'm used to. I will need to rent or purchase a property and one with enough space for my horses and equipment."

"That's right. I'm glad you took the time to look around. I hope you found something that could be suitable for you." Martin and Clara shared the compensation package. It included built-in bonuses for productivity, incentives for innovation, and what amounted to a housing stipend big enough to cover a reasonable rent or mortgage payment for the properties Stella looked at. She wasn't certain she would need a mortgage. When she turned twenty-one, her parents gave her the college money they had saved for her. She invested it well and had savings in the bank from several years' earnings. Her expenses were low, offsetting the modest wages she earned for doing the job she loved.

"Now, before you decide, there is one catch." Clara had been quiet throughout most of the discussion, but this was her time to impress upon her surrogate daughter the need to care for oneself.

"Okay. What's the catch?" Stella was ready to sign on the dotted line before Clara's interjection. Now, she wasn't so certain.

"Well, we are giving you a mandatory paid one week vacation to go home and see your family before you start this new job. We know you haven't seen your folks for two or three years and this new job could keep you out of touch more than ever. This is not negotiable."

"Now that's an interesting twist. I would love to see my family but don't want Jed to be hanging on longer than his wife can tolerate and would hate to leave you here without my replacement. Have you thought of when this vacation should happen?" Stella looked to Clara, then Martin, and then to her hands. Her fingernails stood out, showing signs of work. Some dirt didn't come out with the last cleanup. She needed to make one more pass with the nailbrush before dinner.

"You check with your parents and see what works best for them. It can be next week, the week after, but within the month you should take this trip. If you end up buying a home, it would be a great time to have your parents as a sounding board and such. Now I know you're a proud woman and I have a lot of confidence in your success, but having your parents in your corner is always a good thing, too." Clara worried sometimes that Stella didn't let others in and she may one day find herself in need without a safety net around her.

"I will make that call tomorrow and let you know."

"That's right. Tonight you are busy, aren't you? In fact, from the dust coming up the drive, I think your chariot is on its way. Let's head out and meet him." Martin stood up, held his hand out first to help Clara out of her chair, then to shake hands with Stella. "I'm glad it looks like we have a meeting of the minds."

"Yes, and I think your offer is fair. I haven't done this exact work before, but as I imagine it, the compensation seems right on." Stella was more flattered by the offer than she let on. She forced her attention to the meeting as her mind wanted to wander to the upcoming date. Stella was nervous. Dating didn't come naturally to her. Being one-on-one with the opposite sex with no horse or cow between them frightened her a little.

Brandon saw the group standing on the Drake's front deck and drove up to the front of the house. By the time he hopped out of his pickup, Martin had reached the front of the truck to greet him. Stella looked at Clara and sucked in her breath, eyes wide as a wave of panic passed through her.

Clara grabbed Stella's wrist with her petite hand and their eyes locked. "Just be yourself and have fun. You'll be fine." Stella nodded and flashed a partial grin.

"It's nice to see you lovely ladies this fine afternoon." Brandon leaned in to kiss Clara's cheek. He turned to Stella and held out the crook of his arm. "You look like you might be ready to hit the town, Stella. Is this still a good time for you to go? I don't mean to be interrupting anything here."

"Oh, this is a great time to go. Thanks." Stella turned to her employers. "Thanks for meeting with me. I'll follow up with you soon on those dates."

She turned back to Brandon. "Okay Mr. Cage! Let's find that restaurant I've heard so many good things about, shall we?"

Stella slipped her arm in Brandon's for her escort to the pickup. Martin wrapped his arm around Clara and with his free arm waved Stella and Brandon off. "You kids have fun now, ya hear?"

"Thanks, Martin. We will."

Brandon opened the passenger door for Stella. She wasn't too sure how she felt about that. She never was one to be doted on. Instead, she wanted to be the best version of the guys that she could be. Her mind rotated between her commands to breathe and relax.

Brandon reached his long legs into the

pickup and slid in behind the wheel. "It's nice to see you again, Stella. How have you been?"

Brandon studied Stella's profile before he turned the key. She was beautiful and complex. Her beauty was that of a princess with refined features, dark hair, a perfect smile and flawless sun-kissed skin. He knew she was so much more than her beauty. He was on guard to measure her response to compliments. He sensed that she needed her tough exterior, given the line of work she was in.

"It's been a fantastic week. How about for you?" Stella wasn't ready to share her big news. After all, Brandon was still a relative stranger.

"Yeah, it's been a good week here, too. Busy, like most are, and there was a lot of travel this week so it went by fast."

"Where do you travel?" Stella didn't know much about Brandon's work and didn't recall knowing any lawyers on a personal level.

"Usually I travel to the larger Arizona-based farmers and ranchers. This week I went with a partner to some meetings in California and Colorado. They were agricultural meetings, discussing current events and potential lobbying efforts. It was interesting from a big picture standpoint, but there was still the regular work to do in the evenings."

"I'm not familiar at all with what your work would look like. What is the regular work you had to do on top of traveling and going to meetings?"

"For the lawsuits I'm working on there is legal research to do and a lot of writing for the court, to explain our position and argue on behalf of our clients. Then there is discovery. Are you familiar with that from a lawsuit perspective?"

This was going just the way Stella wanted it to. Keep him talking so she didn't have to reveal much. "I can't say I am."

The trip to the restaurant would take about thirty minutes, Stella estimated. If he kept talking, it would go by fast.

"All the parties in a lawsuit have a right to ask for answers to certain questions to get access to things like documents, videos and other things that support or refute either the allegations the plaintiffs are making, or the defenses being raised by the other party. If you look at it, discovery brings fair play to the litigation; so all parties can put all the necessary information out on the table, so to speak. Posturing, stalling and ego games often overshadow objectivity. I find it frustrating."

"Sorry but you need to break it down for me.

Can you give me an example?" Stella understood the big picture. It sounded like two ranchers fighting over a fence line, neither of them wanting to be wrong and neither one having any real evidence to support their position.

"Sorry, I don't mean to do all the talking here."

"No, that's fine. This is interesting to me. I'm learning something new."

"Okay, if you're sure."

"I am." Stella was certain she wanted him to talk instead of her. The *breathe, relax* mantra was still floating through her mind. Hopefully it would take effect by the time they reached the restaurant. She knew she couldn't avoid talking all night.

"With some attorneys, it becomes the classic standoff. They won't tell you details about their client or their theory of the case. Instead, they put all kinds of pressure on you and your client to produce ridiculous amounts of information. At this stage of litigation, the information being exchanged doesn't have to be the caliber of information that a judge or jury would make their decision on. The discovery rules allow for wide latitude to share information with limited arguments against sharing. So, the other side buries you in all this discovery that you know will never be relevant in the courtroom but you have little opportunity to fight against."

"Well, that hardly seems fair. Is there no way to call it to the judge's attention and have them referee the game?"

"Very good point. When the other side is using the discovery process to harass you or your client, it is possible to go to the court. But generally, they send the attorneys out to the hallway to come to some agreement or they assign a discovery referee to help resolve the dispute. Meanwhile, the parties are spending huge amounts of money because of the gaming going on."

"Have you ever found it was the right thing to do for your client? I mean to bury the other guy in this discovery? Is it useful to buy time or anything like that?"

"On the rare occasion it has been the right thing to do, but it is so unprofessional and against our code of conduct that we – I - try to avoid it at all costs. I try to be reasonable with the other side. I ask for those things I believe we need to test the case and will meet with opposing counsel who has asked for too much and try to get their justification, but some days it feels like a big chess game that goes on and on with no winner."

5

"That was the fastest trip to town I've ever had."

Stella meant it. She always made this trip alone, listening to the radio, making lists in her head of things she had to pick up and things she had to complete when she returned home. It was great to have Brandon as a distraction. She had snuck a few glances at Brandon during the ride when she could study his face. He had a strong jaw and perfectly groomed brown hair. Given his striking good looks, she imaged his parents were a beautiful couple.

"I'm hoping the evening doesn't pass too quickly. I'm looking forward to getting to know you, Stella. I've met no one like you before. Now, let's see if you can get behind the food here at

Casa de Francisco. You might find it old-fashioned and I mean no offense to you at all, but my father taught me to open the car door for a lady. I've done it all my life. Would you allow me the pleasure of opening the door for you?"

"No offense taken. My father taught my brothers the same and I respect them all for it. Happy to wait for you to open my door." *How nice of him to ask. Breathe. Relax.*

Stella had seen smaller restaurants but Brandon was right; Casa de Francisco was on the small side. The owners had repurposed a house as a restaurant with authentic Mexican décor. The host met them at the door and greeted Brandon by name. Brandon introduced Stella to Jose, the son of the owners, who ushered them to a small side room with a private table for two.

"Well Mr. Cage, it appears you've been here before. Is there where you bring all your dates?"

"This restaurant is a family favorite. Jose's parents and mine go back many years. My mother used to buy tamales from his mother when she sold them out of her home. As far as dates go, no. I don't recall bringing a date here. When I was in high school I had two dates, both for prom, and my mother and the girls' mothers orchestrated both. I seem to recall a group of us going out to Outback or Chili's. In college and law school I went out some but didn't date."

"What does that mean?"

Before Brandon could answer, the waitress took their drink orders. Stella usually enjoyed a pull on a whiskey bottle after a long day's work, but she thought refinement in her drinking habits was in order for this evening. She ordered the house margarita. Brandon joined her with the same.

"Well, groups of us would let our hair down at the pub near campus, but I didn't do any one-on-one dating. It just wasn't in the cards for me." Brandon chuckled. "I may seem like a super-smart geek, but I had to study hard to get through school."

"So, now that you've made it through school and you're out in the work world, are you glad you did it? Go to law school, I mean?"

Brandon looked into Stella's eyes and smiled. "Yes, if only because it was an entree for me to meet you."

"Slick, Brandon. I guess I invited that one, didn't I?"

"What? I mean it, Stella. You intrigue me and you are oh, so beautiful. Now, why don't you tell me something about yourself?"

"Thank you for the compliment. I don't hear

that much, thankfully. I mean I don't want my co-workers looking at me that way. If they do, I lose respect. They don't see me as an equal."

"So, how did you come to be a cowboy anyway? I think you have to admit that it's an unusual profession for a woman."

"It is. And there is nothing I would rather be doing. I grew up on a ranch in South Dakota with three brothers. We were all competitive with one another, so from an early age I learned basic cowboy skills. We were in rodeos and raised rodeo livestock. For me, it's a natural fit."

"The girls I knew in school who grew up on a ranch would never have thought to go the cowboy route. They would rather be rodeo queen or a rancher's wife raising kids. I think it's awesome that you've paved your own way into a world you seem to love."

"Yes, I love it. I didn't know what I would do after high school. There was nothing in the college catalog that interested me and the ranch was getting crowded with the boys coming and going and at least two of them planning to start their own places, eventually. I took a road trip and by some circumstance, I landed in New Mexico at a ranch there. The owners took me in and gave me free rein to develop my cowboy skills. It was a real blessing."

"So, how did you get here to Arizona from New Mexico? And with the Drakes? They are such wonderful people."

"They have been a godsend, for sure. I outgrew the job in New Mexico and the owners saw that. They introduced me to Martin and Clara and encouraged me to join them at Winding Slough Ranch. It's been a wonderful three years with them there and I'm ready for a change."

"Oh? I just met you! Are you looking at leaving already?"

"I'm not going far. Martin and Clara offered me a foreman position up at Rabbit Creek Ranch, up north about eighty miles."

"Congratulations. That's quite a promotion for you. Is that on the federal land up there? Martin told me he was running cattle up there."

"That's right. He's had a herd up there for a long time. His foreman has to retire for family reasons, and I feel honored that they would offer me the position. It's going to differ from my usual experience, but I'm looking forward to the challenge."

"I would love to hear more about it when you get into the position. When do you start?"

Stella laughed. "Well, that's a funny story. Clara and Martin are requiring me to take a vacation, to go home and see my family before I can start."

"That's sweet of them. You are probably one to work constantly and not take the time to enjoy yourself. That's my guess."

"You're not too wrong. I love my job. And I love my family too. I haven't been home for two or three years and it would be great to visit. I appreciate their position. I squirm a bit at the thought of being forced to do it, but I'll get over that and enjoy it. Tomorrow I'll call my mom and see when they are available. They travel some so it could be right away, or not."

Dinner arrived and was a welcome reprieve for Stella. She had talked more about herself than she wanted already and she needed a breather.

"Look at this plate! It's overflowing with food. It looks wonderful." Stella looked at the waitress. "Thank you!"

"Can I get either of you anything else?"

"Stella, would you care to join me in another drink or a glass of wine?"

"Sure. I'll have whatever you're having." Wine didn't seem the right drink to combine with the meal before her, but another margarita seemed too sweet and overkill. Brandon ordered them each a Paloma. Stella hoped it would be less sweet than the margarita. And it was.

"I hope someday you will invite me up to see Rabbit Creek Ranch. I am interested in learning all the variations on livestock operations. It's my hope to study and support ranchers of diverse backgrounds with many styles and sizes of ranch operations."

Brandon secretly dreamed of a higher profile political position. One day… but he had a lot to learn before that and his sophomoric ideas of better ways of doing business needed to evolve and grow through the tutelage of operators and lawmakers who went before him. It also interested him to learn how other countries support their farmers and ranchers, which Brandon saw as the backbone of the American way.

"Well, we shall see. I have to learn my way around and get somewhat of a schedule established. Besides, anything I know you can learn through Martin." It wasn't Stella's nature to be a naysayer, but for her it was premature to make any future promises, even if he premised it on business and not personal matters.

"True, true. As the one closest to the work, however, you may have input in addition to what Martin could share."

"This is the best Mexican food I have ever

eaten. Thank you so much for bringing me here. It's a nice change from the casseroles and such that I get at the ranch." Stella caught herself. She didn't want Brandon to think she was un-happy with Clara and the ranch. She put her fork down, folded her hands in her lap and looked at Brandon. "I mean it's nice for a change. Clara's a great cook."

Brandon looked up from his dinner and chuckled. "Oh, I know what you mean. Don't forget, I grew up on a big ranch too and I would venture a guess and say that Clara's cookbook and my mom's are cut from the same cloth. They know how to stretch a few cans of food and a package of burger, whether it be beef, pork, chicken, or turkey, to feed a small army."

"I suppose my mom could be their sister. She fed our entire town over the years, and several drifters too, besides our family and our hands. Branding parties were always a big party at our place, fiddles and all, after the branding was over. Mom made a big deal out of the meals, and at the end we had a pig roast or a lamb roast and invited the neighbors and many from town."

Stella drifted back to those days when they had big parties. In her early years, Yvette rele-gated Stella to the kitchen to help prepare and serve, but as she approached her teens, she rebelled and refused to come in from her work alongside the men. The soreness and sense of accomplishment she got from sorting, roping, and wrestling was much more satisfying to her ego.

"Sounds like your mom went all out. We were much less of a party bunch, I would say. Not that we didn't have fun. We did. But it was all Mom could do to feed the essential hands and family, with no extras."

"Yeah, I think I come from a long line of party planners. My grandparents never had much, but they always found food to share and invited groups of people home." A winter scene flashed in Stella's memory while a smile crept over her lips. She looked up to see Brandon grinning.

"It looks like there's more to that story. Care to share?" Stella had a tough exterior, but there was a familiarity Brandon felt with her energy. She reminded him of stories he heard about his own mother from her younger days. She was a tomboy, who worked alongside his father from the beginning of their lives together.

"I was just thinking of how my parents, my mother really, took over Christmas for the town. About twenty years ago she talked my father into giving hayrides and sleigh rides for several weekends leading up to Christmas. It was her way of seeing all her friends and their out-of-town guests coming to celebrate the holidays. They took up donations for a charity, served hot drinks and cookies. The local newspaper offered their photographer to take photos, so long as they could use some in the paper."

Brandon's eyebrows shot up, his eyes wide, and a grin took over his face. "Now that is a party! One I'd like to see someday. That's an impressive undertaking. Do they still do it?"

"Oh yes, without fail. If ever you're in Buffalo Ridge, South Dakota between Thanksgiving and Christmas, I highly recommend it as THE place to be." Stella smiled back at Brandon then took a drink of her Paloma. She found herself at ease with Brandon. More so than she thought she would be.

After dinner, the two drove back to Winding Slough Ranch. They shared stories of their childhoods and laughed at their own, and each other's stories.

As they drove into the yard, Stella directed Brandon to her bunkhouse. She was the only occupant. Being the only female cowboy, Clara insisted that she have her own quarters.

Brandon parked and walked around to open the door for Stella. "This has been the highlight of my week…no, my year, Stella. I enjoyed my-self more tonight than I imagined I could."

"I have to admit, I wasn't sure I could relax into a date, it's been so long. But you made it easy, Brandon. I enjoyed myself and have to say, the food and drinks were superb."

"Does that mean you might like to try it again sometime?" Brandon was hopeful. He took her by the elbow and guided her up the boardwalk to the bunkhouse.

"I would. I cannot promise when I might be available again, but I will keep you posted." They arrived at her door. Stella turned to look at Brandon. The moonlight cast a glow on him, il-luminating his flawless face, kind eyes and per-fect smile.

"I will anxiously await details of your sched-ule. I have some travel of my own coming up. I would love to see you again before you head up north, but if not, I'm happy to make the trip up to see you there." Brandon paused and looked deep into Stella's eyes. He firmly planted his feet. He wanted to stay; yet he didn't expect Stella to invite him in. This was, after all, their first date and her parents raised her to be a proper woman. Her eyes held his.

"I think I had better call it a night Brandon.

I'm sure we could talk all night, but let's save some for the next time, okay?"

"I like that idea." Brandon slowly retrieved his keys. As his hand came out of his pocket, he raised it to give Stella a hug. They embraced, the moon shining down on them. Stella wondered if Clara and Martin were watching from their porch where they enjoyed an evening cocktail, sometimes late into the evening as they watched the stars dancing in the night sky. As the thought passed, she eased into the hug, drinking in the warmth and strength of the handsome Brandon Cage.

6

———

"Hey Mom, what's wrong?" Yvette awakened Stella with her call.

"Nothing's wrong. I just wanted to reach you before you headed out for the day. So… how was the date?"

"Seriously Mom? It's four in the morning and you're asking me about my date? You're so funny!"

"Well, it's not like we've had many of these chats and none in recent years."

"That's true. It was lovely. Brandon Cage is a very nice man."

"Tell me. Did you laugh? Did you relax?" Yvette knew her daughter too well. She was a driven young woman and rarely stopped to smell the roses on life's journey.

"Yes, and yes. We could have spent days swapping stories… about our families. They brought lots of laughs."

"Um, okay. I'm not sure how to take that but I'm glad there was laughing, even if it was at my expense."

"Well, it seems his mother could be your twin party planner, Mom."

"I'd love to meet her. Maybe someday."

"Whoa! Let's not rush things. First things first. I need to talk to you about something else."

"Okay honey. What's up?" Stella had a slight tone of concern in her voice.

"Well, I'm being promoted, and it's a neat opportunity but there's a catch."

"Oh, what's the catch?"

"Before I can start the new job, I have a mandatory vacation to Buffalo Ridge. Martin and Clara know it's been a couple of years since I've been home, and they would like me to take a trip before I take on this new position. I will have less flexibility to schedule time off after I move."

"You're coming home? When? Oh, wait 'til I tell your dad and brothers!"

"When is up to you. Are you guys going to be home for a while or are you traveling?"

"Let me look at my calendar. We're not going anywhere in the next two weeks, but let me see. Our next trip is to look at some livestock in Nebraska, but that's not for over a month from now."

"When would it be convenient for me to come? The sooner the better for me since I can't change jobs until after my vacation."

"Tomorrow isn't soon enough for me dear, but you do whatever is best for you."

"How about I shoot for one week from now?"

"Sure, sure Stella. That sounds great! I'll let everyone know and we'll have a dinner party. Your old friend Kelly Brown is still around. She's married now, to Tom Schuler, and they are expecting a baby. I'll invite them and our neighbors, the Johnstons and Wilders and…"

"Wait. Mom, can we please just keep it to family and not plan things? This is my vacation and I just love hanging out with you guys at the ranch. Maybe ride the Badlands and check out your new rodeo stock. Please?" Stella pled. She knew she was forcing her mom to break all her instincts, but she needed this downtime before moving.

"Sure, honey. Whatever works for you."

"Thanks, Mom. That means a lot to me."

"Okay, now tell me about this new job."

"Yeah. Martin and Clara have a ranch up

north, the Rabbit Creek Ranch. It's a different kind of ranch. There is no ranch house. I will get my own place to live."

"Well, I just don't understand that, at all. How can it be a ranch?"

"Martin runs the cattle on federal land. I will be out on the ranch a lot with them. There are some temporary quarters out on the grazing lands and some outbuildings for supplies, but there won't be cattle in my backyard like normal ranches."

"So, you'll be out with the cattle and then come home at night?"

"No, not really. I will stay out on the trail with the cattle some. I will move them and tend to them in the high desert. It really is a different way of ranching, but there's a special market for the cattle that graze in these pasturelands, living on whatever the desert throws at them. It's fascinating, really. It's amazing to see how they survive in what we would think of as harsh conditions, but they do, and they do it well. There's impressive stock."

"I think you will have to tell me more about it when you visit. I'm not really picturing where you are going to be sleeping and eating and what about the wild animals out there? How many men will you have with you?"

"If I had my druthers, I would have an all-female crew but the real answer is that sometimes I will be alone, just me and my satellite phone. Other times I will have hired hands to help me with the drive. Yes, we can talk about it more when I come home and I will have more answers. I'll be looking for a place up there this week."

"This sounds very exciting for you. Do you have any pictures of the area you can share with us? I imagine it's beautiful."

"It is, and I did snap some on my phone when I was up there to visit recently. I'll show you when I'm home."

"Great! Well, it seems like we talked about a lot in just a few minutes. I am so excited to see you, and soon!"

"I better get my reservations made. I've got today to do some house hunting and get things rolling. Thanks for calling Mom."

STELLA JUMPED OUT OF BED. She felt the effects of the heavy meal and drinks from the night before. She rushed to the kitchen of the large bunkhouse to fill her travel mug with Clara's strong hot coffee. The coffee pot was on an automatic timer that started brewing at half-past four every morning. Clara wouldn't be in the kitchen until six, thankfully. Stella wasn't ready for another inquisition. One mother hen this early in the morning was enough.

As she drank her coffee, she did a quick online search for ranchettes near Rabbit Creek Ranch. Jed let her know via text that he and his wife were leaving their home and would put it up for sale. His wife needed to be closer to the doctors in the city. Jed's house was larger than she wanted. They raised a large family there, and his wife worked in the kitchen at the elementary school so they had two incomes.

Stella wanted something simple and affordable. She had enough money to buy something small, with a large down payment and manageable monthly mortgage payments. She also considered financing through her parents and planned to approach that subject when she was visiting Buffalo Ridge Ranch. They had offered before but she didn't need it until now. It made her a little queasy to think of being that entangled with them. She cherished the privacy she created by being so far from home.

The online search yielded seven properties with two bedrooms. She crossed three off the list. They had too little property for her horses.

She needed Ranger and Molly to be comfortable. A fourth property piqued her interest. It was a converted shipping container with two bedrooms and just over seven hundred square feet. She put it on the list to drive by despite fears the metal would attract heat in the summer.

The three remaining properties were within her budget and had adequate land. They were built in the 1970s and 1980s. The online pictures showed them all to be in good condition. She sent messages to the respective realtors, hoping to see properties the same day. She snapped pictures of the addresses and gathered a notebook and pen. It was only a two-hour drive, but she wanted to become acclimated with the area so she planned to have breakfast at a diner in Watson.

Stella was halfway to Watson when she heard a text message land in her phone. She would check it later. Right now she needed to concentrate on the task at hand. The landscape of the lower desert gave way to some steep inclines where trees were sparse and boulders plentiful. Stella felt closer to the clouds as she drove deeper into the high desert. *A new frontier to conquer.*

She drove into the small town she targeted

for house hunting. It was early on a Sunday morning, and the small town was lazy. There were four cars at the diner, two of which seemed to belong to the lone cook and only waitress who greeted her with a cheery welcome.

"Good mornin' darlin'! Welcome to Maxine's. I'm Edna and I'll be serving you today. Will anyone be joining you this morning?" The waitress looked around Stella through the glass front door to see if anyone was coming in behind her.

"No, ma'am. It's just me this morning. Do you mind if I have a booth?"

"Well, I don't know, we're pretty busy." The waitress gave Stella a stern look then laughed. "Ha! It's Sunday morning. We won't be busy until the services are over. You just point out the booth you want, and if you're still here at half-past nine I'll have to kick you out."

"Fair enough. I promise to be quick." Stella and the waitress exchanged chuckles. If Edna's personality was a sign of the community, Stella knew she would like it here.

"Here's a menu. We have biscuits and gravy this morning for $3.95. That's our every Sunday special. Coffee for you this morning?"

"Coffee, black, please. How on earth do you

sell biscuits and gravy for $3.95 without losing your shirts?"

"Well now, aren't you the smart one? Truth is, very few people order them. Somehow, they got a bad name from the health and fitness gurus, so it's a safe bet for us. Now, don't let me scare you off. They're good and they're cheap. Old Hal back there in the kitchen has been making them for about twenty-five years here, every Sunday. Used to be a better seller."

"Oh, I believe you, but today I'm in the mood for a big fat egg scramble with potatoes. Do you make anything like that?"

"You're the kind of gal I like… one who knows what she wants. We have what we call Chickens in the Potato Patch. The chef scrambles the eggs and adds onions and peppers, bacon and country potatoes."

"That's it. Perfect!"

"Well now, here's the tricky part. You have to choose what else you want with it."

"There's more?"

"That's right. You can have a pancake… buttermilk, multigrain or blueberry or you can have a baking powder biscuit or toast… wholewheat, sourdough or white."

"I will try your blueberry pancake."

"Sounds great. You won't regret it." Edna

pulled her wrist toward her face to look at her watch. "But I'm not sure you will make my deadline."

Stella laughed. "Listen. This girl knows how to eat and run. If I didn't I couldn't survive. Don't you worry about me."

Edna smiled back. It was nice to have such easy banter before the big crowd came in. "Will there be anything else?"

"A tall glass of orange juice, please. I brought my travel mug in. Can I get a coffee refill in this before I go?"

"Certainly. Let me put a fresh pot on so there's plenty when you're ready."

"Thanks, Edna." Stella's words fell on Edna's backside as she rushed off to do her work.

With breakfast ordered, Stella could now check her messages. She picked up the phone and saw the text message from earlier. It was Brandon. Stella sucked in her breath as she opened the message. She was focused on travel plans, house hunting and the new job; there was no time to dwell on the evening with Brandon. She surprised herself.

Good morning, Stella. Thank you for last night. I haven't had such a good time since... never. I look forward to seeing you again. Good luck with your travel arrangements and house hunting.

Stella let her mind wander to their date. She smiled and felt a little flip in her stomach. She had enjoyed herself. Maybe there was hope that someone would understand her and be a good fit. She wasn't certain Brandon was it. He felt a little too slick to her. Maybe it was his perfect haircut and pressed clothes. He seemed a little showy. She shook her head and silently scolded herself. *"Give the guy a chance. You've only had one date."*

There was an advantage to being early and one of a very few customers in a diner - the speed with which food arrived. Edna set two plates in front of Stella. One held a huge blueberry pancake. The other was heaped with eggs and potatoes. "Here you are, miss."

"Stella. I'm Stella and you may see me around here more. I'm looking at some properties up here. Thinking of moving in."

"Nice to meet you, Stella. Now, why on earth would you move here to Watson? We're the last place people go before they fall into that big hole in the ground a few hours east of here. You know what I mean?"

"I'm coming up for work."

"You work for the government, or what?"

"No. I'm a cowboy. I manage livestock and

will work up on the federal lands over a little east of here."

"A cowboy, huh? You sure don't look like any cowboy I ever dated."

Stella laughed. "Well, that's a good thing, right?"

"Yes ma'am, it is. I mean you're pretty and all, but I like my cowboys a little more… uh, shall we say, rugged?"

"I understand completely. Let's just say that I'm a girl who does a cowboy's job."

"Interesting. I bet there's a story behind that. So, Stella, if you're going to be around these parts, maybe you can tell me about it someday. I mean, how you became a cowboy."

"Sure thing, Edna. One day we can hit the bar after work and I'll tell you all about it. There is a bar in this town, right?"

"Oh yeah, we got three of them. But honey, you come on over to my house. We can hang out on the deck, watch the squirrels and drink for free. I just get myself in trouble when I hang out at the bar."

"Sounds like you have your own story to tell, eh Edna?"

"Well, maybe. You come to see me when you get situated. Where are you looking to live?"

"I'm looking on the east side of town, close

as I can get to my work. I have to have land enough for my horses so I can't be in town."

"There are a few places for sale over there. Seems most of them were recreation places for city folk who wanted to get out of the heat down south. I'm sure you'll find just the right thing. You enjoy your breakfast now." Edna tapped her watch with her finger. "Clock's a-ticking girlie."

"Yes, ma'am. I'm on it." Stella grabbed the syrup and prepared her pancake. After the heavy meal last night, the quantity of food in front of her now seemed overwhelming. She would be lucky to get half of it eaten. She took a bite of the blueberry pancake and smiled. It was just like the ones her mom made, light and fluffy with big juicy blueberries. She would be happy to come back and eat this on Sunday mornings.

7

____

Stella met with a realtor who represented two of the properties on her list. They could not get into the third property, but Stella drove by it. It was closest to Rabbit Creek Ranch and the highest-priced of the properties. From what Stella could see it offered more acres of land than the others, but much of that land was unusable due to an incline and large boulders. For the extra money, she would stick with one of the other properties.

The property that topped her list was unusual. The couple that had it built in the 1970s used it as a summer home initially, but stopped coming when they got older. Most recently, it was a vacation rental. The couple's son marketed it and a local woman managed the housekeeping for them. Ponderosa pine lined the horizon along the outside edge of the ten acres. There was an outbuilding for tack with a lean-to to shelter the horses. The truck and horse trailer would easily fit in the two-stall garage with an extended area used for a workshop. The house was red and built in the style of a barn. A river rock fireplace stood at the center of the home. One could stoke the fire from the kitchen and dining area or the living room. The owners had decorated it as a turn-of-the-century style home. It was furnished with beautiful antiques, including a working antique cook stove in mint condition. All would be included in the sale.

This house was move-in ready, with a few changes that would make it more suitable for Stella. She would take down the shelves that lined the living room and dining room, removing the large collection of plates and antique pitchers. The realtor suggested that, with some clutter removed, the home would feel more spacious than its fifteen hundred square feet. The two bedrooms were large, with the bonus of a second bathroom in the master bedroom. The owners advertised the master bedroom as a 'honeymoon suite' in the vacation rental brochure.

Stella also liked the second lower-priced house five miles west of the first one on Trail

Water Loop. The sellers had recently remodeled. It had high ceilings, contemporary light paint, an open floor plan and a sweet wrap-around porch. It reminded Stella of a mini version of the Buffalo Ridge Ranch home. The drawback of this home was the lack of a garage. If she got it for the right price, however, she could have a garage built. There was no shelter for the horses, only a tack shack. This property had slightly less land, but it was enough for her two horses to graze and exercise.

The realtor had her work cut out for her, though. Stella decided to low-ball the first house on her list. "I think the sellers have added a fifty-thousand dollar sentimental value to their property. I will make an offer for that amount lower than the asking price."

The realtor put her pen down. They were sitting at the soda fountain of a local gas station to discuss Stella's thoughts on the houses.

"I'm familiar with these sellers and I will guess that they won't budge and they won't counter your offer."

"That's fine." Stella answered firmly. "Their home has been on the market for over two hundred days. If they are ready to sell it, they will have to be reasonable in their asking price."

"I get your point and I don't disagree with

you. I'm just telling you what my experience with them has been. Their attorney son from California strongly influences them."

"Well, that's my position. As I say, the second house at $20,000 under asking price, or even this other one that we didn't see today would work for me. I'm not married to the nostalgia in that house. In fact, it will take some work to make it fit my personality, including changing all those bright yellow walls to something calmer."

"I'll put in the offer tomorrow. I'm sure there won't be another bidder today."

"That's fine with me. In the meantime, could you get me a little more information on that new listing on Juniper Lane? I think the only drawback I saw was that it had only one bathroom. I would be curious to know if there's a way to put a second bath in. The price is low enough that I could invest something if it has everything else I need."

Stella knew that a perfect property would show up soon, even if it wasn't one she saw with the realtor. If all else failed, she could find a short-term rental and keep looking.

IT WAS time to turn to more pressing matters. She had not responded to Brandon, and she had not completed her travel plans.

She looked out the single window of the bunkhouse and spotted Martin crossing the yard. Quickly, she pulled her boots on and ran out to greet him.

"Hey Stella, how was your day? You went up north, right?"

"That's right. It was informative and promising. I'll find something, I'm sure. I'm just not positive it was what I saw today. Seems some people get really attached to their things and their home and want me to pay a sentimental tax."

Martin laughed. "I've seen that before, especially if the owner built the home or did major renovations themselves. Sometimes, that's the worst workmanship, but boy, they put their blood, sweat, and tears in the place so it has added value to them."

"That's it exactly! That's what I saw today. It was actually a little sad. I mean, that they are so unrealistic. In one case, the house has been on the market for many months and it's overpriced about fifty grand. Either they are motivated to sell, or they aren't."

"It does sound like you learned a lot about

the area up there. Are there plenty of proper-ties that have accommodations for your horses?"

"Sure. All of them I looked at today did."

"Great. I'm sure something will come up. So what about your vacation? Have you reached your folks?"

"I did. If it's okay with you, I will go next weekend and stay for one week. My mother is already planning meals and has her grocery list written out. She's got my sheets in the washer and told my brothers, Steve and Jesse, who live there."

Martin smiled. "She loves you."

"Yes, she surely does, and as always she uses food to show it. She cooks with so much love you can hardly taste the tomato paste."

Martin nodded toward the home she shared with Clara. "I've seen that pattern before." They laughed.

"I… I don't know if it's okay for me to ask, but did you have a good time last night?"

Stella brought her hand to her forehead and furrowed her brow. "Oh Martin I did. I did. I've just been so caught up with everything going on that I haven't even responded to Brandon's mes-sage from this morning. I enjoyed the food and the company. I'm not sure this is the right time for me to be meeting someone new, but we'll see what happens."

"Yeah, the timing seems a little unfortunate with you moving up north and all, but you're always welcome here if you decide to come back and visit. Clara has adopted you, and frankly, she expects you to visit. When I first mentioned offering you the job she didn't speak to me for two days. She likes having you here. She says it balances the place out. Say, you don't know any other women cowboys looking for a job, do you?"

"I might know a couple and I'll reach out to them. That's another thing to think about here. I had it in the back of my mind that an all-female crew up north may be a good way for me to go."

"That might be a great idea."

"I got that idea from something Jed said. He warned me to choose my hands carefully because they may not all have the same work ethic I do, if you know what I mean."

"I do and I think you're right to keep your mind open. See, I knew you were the best person for this job. You're already shaking things up." Martin put an arm around Stella as the two of them walked toward the bunkhouse kitchen. "Now, shall we see what Clara stirred up for dinner?"

MOST OF THE crew was eating dinner. Those hands who went away for the weekend or spent the weekend resting up all showed up for Sunday dinner. Clara encouraged it by making favorite meals to entice the guys to be back at the ranch at a decent hour. Martin and Clara always joined them for Sunday dinner. It helped fill their need for family. They caught up on everyone's family and comings and goings. They were slow to judge others and encouraged all to be their best selves, even if doing so took them away from the ranch for other endeavors.

"Well Duane, did Rosie accept?" Last week Duane had shown Clara the ring he bought for his sweetheart. It was Rosie's birthday and Duane proposed. Stella had met Rosie once when she visited the ranch, a sweet girl and very young like Duane.

"Yes ma'am, she sure did." The baby-faced cowboy grinned from ear to ear.

Clara clapped her hands and walked around the table to give Duane a big hug. "Oh, I knew she would! I don't know what you were so nervous about."

The group at the table erupted with congratulations and well wishes.

"Do you have a date set yet for the wedding?" Martin asked.

"No, sir. Rosie has three more semesters of college. I want her to finish those before there's a wedding. I've had too many friends that got overwhelmed with all the planning stuff and they quit school and never went back. I'm not the book-learning sort myself, but Rosie, she's really smart and will make a great teacher."

"Now that's great thinking Duane." Martin put his arm around Clara. "We're darn proud of you Duane and happy to see you so doggone happy. Invite Rosie out sometime and we'll throw a party for you both."

"Thank you, sir. I will do that." Duane came from a one-parent family in the area. His father died in a car accident when Duane was a small boy, and his mother never remarried. He looked up to Martin as a father figure and, at times like this, was beyond grateful that he worked for Martin and Clara.

Stella, too, was grateful to the couple that took her in and encouraged her to define and follow her dreams. Her reward seemed to be just around the corner. Never before had she anticipated an opportunity that would allow her to be a cowboy full-time and have her own place. This was beyond her dreams. It was time to build bigger dreams!

After dinner, Stella returned to her bunkhouse and responded to Brandon.

It's been an eventful day. Property search was promising, if not for today for the near future. Made plans to leave next Saturday for a week. Hope you had a great Sunday.

The late Saturday night and long Sunday had tired Stella out. She fell asleep as the news played in the background.

8

Stella filled the week before vacation with her last cattle sorting at Winding Slough Ranch. Her skills were well-suited for this job. She was steady, calm and read the behavior of the cattle well. She was a natural leader for the small crew working with her.

Throughout the day she checked her phone for updates from the realtor. Mid-afternoon she got her first text back.

Offer rejected. Seller offended. No counteroffer.

Stella exhaled a big sigh of relief. The more she thought about the quaint and charming place, the more she realized the romance of the home momentarily captivated her. It was impractical to live with the turn-of-the-century decor and appliances. The place was best used as a novel rest stop for newlyweds and vacationers. She responded to the realtor.

Good. Make offer on Trail Water as we discussed. Any more info on place on Juniper Lane?

Stella knew this offer was also a long shot but she might get lucky enough to find a motivated seller. Heck, they may even come back and say they have a way to get a discounted garage. Stranger things had happened.

Brandon texted later in the afternoon. *Thinking of you. Know you have a busy week. You come back from SD Sat or Sun next weekend? Have time for coffee or dinner when you return?*

Stella smiled. It was nice to have someone thinking about her. She thought about his question and how busy she was. Finally, she decided she could squeeze one more thing in; she wondered if he could. He would have to go back to Phoenix on Sunday night or Monday morning for work, she presumed. That's over a two-hour drive. She needed to be in Watson to look at properties again, which would add another two hours for him.

Return Sat pm. How about breakfast on Sunday in Watson? Pick you up on the way?

Brandon didn't hesitate with his response. Within minutes he committed to going with her and designated a meeting place. Stella smiled and shook her head. She was taking a relative stranger house hunting! There was time to back out if she started feeling uneasy about him joining her. It would be awkward for him to be part of making decisions for the next big step in her life. The more she thought about her impulsive invitation, the more she questioned her ability to think clearly with all the moving parts in her life.

She turned her attention to the work before her. This was no time to allow herself to be distracted. They were finishing up the last push for the day to get the cattle sorted and penned. She would drive some to new grazing land the following day. Truckers would haul others to the stock sale next week. With a herd as large as that of this ranch, culling was a constant process to preserve the integrity of the herd.

They wrapped up the day and headed for dinner. It was after seven, and Clara was ready for them with a hot meal. Clara sat beside her, watching as Stella pushed food around her plate, swirling mashed potatoes around a pile of peas.

"Stella, dear, you haven't eaten tonight. Is there something wrong with the food?" Clara knew Stella well. She could out-eat the men after a long day's work, like today.

"Oh, no! I mean, I don't think so. Sorry,

Clara, I'm distracted with everything that's going on."

"Oh honey, you're such a worrier. Everything will be just fine. You watch and see. Stop worrying so much and eat your dinner. You have another hard day tomorrow and will need your strength." Clara paused so Stella could take a bite. "How is your house search going?"

"Considering I just started, I think it's going well. I've never been through this process before, and it's a little bit hectic. On one hand, the realtor is pushing me to put an offer in because the process takes a while. On the other hand, the offer I'm willing to make is not what the seller wants. I folded on the first house I liked, and in retrospect it would have been an impulse buy and not something that really suited me."

"Well see, that worked out for the best then. I'm sure there would be someplace to rent or you could take the camper up there by the outbuildings at the entrance to the rangeland if you needed to, at least short term. It's all going to be okay." Clara sat in silence while Stella ate more of her dinner, washing it down with coffee.

"Martin said you're going home to see your family this weekend. I'm so happy for you and I bet that news thrilled your momma."

"Oh Clara, you know her too well."

"I only know what you tell me, dear."

"Well, she wanted to plan dinner parties and such. I had to put the brakes on her. I need to relax, stay low key. I want to wear my pajamas until noon, drink coffee and eat cinnamon rolls if I want. I want a glass of wine on the deck, looking out over the beautiful Badlands in the evening, swapping stories with my brothers. Getting all dolled up and going into town isn't high on my priority list."

"I understand. I also know why your mom wants to prance around town with you. She's got to be so proud of you. You're such a beautiful woman and look at all you've accomplished! You've made this unique life that others can't even dream of. You have work you love and a surrogate family here that loves you. Stella, you know I will miss you when you move up north. I hope you're looking for at least a two-bedroom place. Can I visit you?"

"Yes, Clara, and I'm looking for a place where you can have your own bathroom and even a decent kitchen, in case you get inspired to cook for me." Stella smiled and reached out to hug Clara. She pulled back and looked into Clara's face. "I will miss you too but I'll only be about two hours away and you can come to visit anytime."

"And, I will, missy, so you had better mean it!" Clara stood and picked up Stella's now clean plate.

"I do Clara, honestly. Thanks for the chat. I'm going to hit the bunk. Another big day tomorrow. Thanks for dinner."

Clara nodded and walked off to start the dishes. Stella wanted to offer her assistance but when she did that in her early days at the ranch, Clara sternly told her it was her job and that Stella had already put in her day's work. Instead, Stella told the other hands goodnight and headed to her own tiny bunkhouse. It was large enough only for a twin-sized bunk bed and small dresser with a portable television on top, one chair, a mini-fridge with a microwave on top and a small bathroom with a sink in a foot-wide counter, and a camper-size shower.

Stella popped two ice cubes from the tray in the mini-fridge freezer into a glass and poured two fingers of whiskey. She washed up and changed into her pajamas. She turned the television on, mostly for background noise. Looking around, she realized how little space she needed. She lived a compact life. She could be the poster child for the minimalist community. She didn't even have a closet. Her clothes hung on hangers from the foot rail of the top bunk.

Stella downed the whiskey, brushed her teeth, and sank down onto the bed for a good night's sleep. She checked her phone one last time for messages. There were none.

***

THE REST of the week was filled with long days of cowboying. Dinner each night was late and rushed. Finally, very early Saturday morning, she filled her backpack with an assortment of essentials, three t-shirts and two pairs of jeans. As an afterthought, she grabbed a western dress shirt and stuffed in the backpack. She hoped not to need it.

She drove herself to the city to catch the plane. There was no sense in having someone else make the four-hour round-trip drive to drop her off and pick her up again. She found a parking lot coupon to ease the pain of the parking fee. She had learned to be frugal over the years, and now that she was buying a house she was grateful for every penny she had squirreled away.

The flight was uneventful. The reception at the airport was noisy and joyful. Her mom, dad and two brothers greeted her. She arrived around lunchtime, so the group went to a family favorite restaurant before heading out to Buffalo Ridge Ranch.

The week went quickly, and on Stella's terms. Yvette asked Stella twice to go to town and meet up with the coffee ladies. Stella agreed to go the first time but passed on the second. Instead, she checked livestock with her dad. She enjoyed time with her brothers, getting caught up on their lives. The three siblings rode through the Badlands like they did in their younger days. By the end of the week, Stella was relaxed and ready to tackle the next phase of her life, with its twists and turns and unexpected guests.

The sellers of the second property accepted her low-ball offer. They didn't even counter offer. They agreed that a garage was essential; previous feedback had been the same. The wife's uncle was a local contractor and agreed, as a side deal, to build a garage for a discounted price; he could start within two weeks.

With this great news, Stella canceled her trip to Watson with Brandon on Sunday. Once the house deal came in, she decided the trip wasn't necessary and that decision lowered her stress. She would eventually have to go up and sign papers, but that couldn't be done on Sunday. Stella secured a modest family loan with minimal interest from her parents and would pay cash for her house. That sped up the closing process immensely. She could move and start at her new job in three weeks.

It relieved Jed to get the news. *I know you hustled to make this happen so fast. My wife thanks you. She is in the hospital. We sold our house and have found a new one to buy. Timing is perfect.*

Brandon was disappointed their date was canceled but happy that Stella had found a place that would work for her near Watson. *House hunting on a second date could have been interesting, but I'm happy you secured a house you want. Can I see you anyway?*

Stella couldn't do any business until Monday, so all she had to do on Sunday was laundry and getting organized for the workweek. She would like to see Brandon but not all day, and she didn't want to stay on the ranch after traveling all week.

Want to come to the ranch? We can take the horses out for a ride in the Ponderosas. They need their legs stretched after my vacation.

Stella didn't doubt that Brandon knew his way around a horse, but she wanted to see how he handled himself. She didn't mean to be testing him, however some things were really important to her, like how others treated animals.

Sounds great. I'll bring coffee and breakfast? See you at 8?

Great. One less decision for Stella to make. Starting early would help them avoid the midday heat, and he could get to Phoenix at a decent hour.

Perfect. See you then.

Stella checked one more thing off her list of things to do. She hated structuring her life to this extent, where she wrote lists to make sure she didn't miss anything important. With so many things going on though, it helped manage inner anxiety so she could perform her best at work. It was something she had seen her mother do. During the visit home, she found she had more similarities with her mother than she ever knew before. They have similar tastes in food, movies, books, and music. One evening, as the two cleaned up after dinner and nursed their wine, they discovered their taste in men was identical too.

"The things I love most about your father are his humility, integrity, love for family, nature and the livestock. He has drive that grounds him yet he is innovative. He's really an awesome man and always has been. His parents raised a great human."

"Gramps and Grams were like that too."

"That's right. He did not get his great traits and handsome looks from the dirt. They deserve all the credit."

"I think it helps that you always see the best in him and help him shine, Mom. You've been a wonderful wife and mother."

"Well thank you, Stella. You could never give me a better compliment. Those are my passions and I always try to do my best." Yvette handed a large pan to Stella to dry. Turning back to the sink, she looked into the soap bubbles as if they were tealeaves at the bottom of a cup. "Will you ever want those things, Stella? I mean…to be a wife and mother?"

"I've avoided thinking about those things, Mom. But now, as I look at graduating from my training grounds on the ranch and getting my own home and being essentially my own day-to-day boss, I am more open to the idea that my life is meant for more. Look at you. You are the ultimate role model and I know that if I got over-whelmed, you would put everything down and come running to help me."

"Darn straight I would." Yvette smiled at her

daughter and nodded. "These boys can fend for themselves."

"You taught them well. The boys have been cooking and doing laundry since grade school. They used to think it was punishment. Now they know better."

"What about you, Stella? Have you thought about what you want in a man, if he were to be your husband and the father of your children?"

"A little, yeah and honestly, he would be like Dad. I would have to have a man with integrity, who respected me and saw me as an equal partner in life. He would have to be ambitious and generous, family-oriented, thoughtful about people and nature and not harsh."

"Well, have you met anyone like that?"

"Wait. I have one more thing to add. He has to handle a horse and treat animals right. That's an absolute must for me."

"So, is there anyone you know like that yet?"

"We'll see. I'm getting Brandon out to the ranch for a ride. He doesn't know it yet, but it's my little test."

9

―――――――

Brandon hopped out of the truck and reached back in to pull out two to-go containers of breakfast and coffee, just as promised. Stella met him at the truck with a relaxed grin, ready to ride.

"Well, good morning sunshine! You look refreshed from your vacation."

"Good morning! I have to admit that I am refreshed and eager for the next few weeks to pass so I can get on with my newest adventure." She reached for a coffee and took a sip. It had cooled perfectly on the trip from town.

"Let's take these into the dining room." Stella pointed to the main bunkhouse. "My bunkhouse is just a little too small for two of us.

You would have to eat lying down on the top bunk."

"The kitchen sounds great." On Sunday mornings Clara didn't cook. Coffee was always on but, outside of toast and hot water for oatmeal, the food came from the refrigerator or cupboard. The dining hall was quiet.

"I have here two breakfast burritos, one with sausage and the other with bacon. What's your preference?"

"Today seems like a bacon kind of day. Thank you very much."

"You are welcome. There is hot sauce and salsa in the bag if you like."

"Great. Would you like orange juice?" Stella got up to get orange juice from the refrigerator and grabbed one for him, too.

"This is a fantastic burrito. When I went to Watson, I stopped into this neat little diner and met a new friend."

"Is that right? It sounds like a friendly place."

"Edna was friendly. She invited me to her place to swap stories when I get moved in."

"So, are you getting excited about your house and moving?"

"Surprisingly, I am. I've never been one to accumulate things and have enjoyed the freedom of not being tied down to property but, as with all things in life, change happens. I'm ready now for this change, both in my home and my job."

"That's great."

"Yeah, and enough about me. How have you been? Has work been busy for you?"

"I had a fantastic week at work. We had meetings in southern California during the first part of the week. Every day I learn something new about the field of agricultural law and it all fascinates me. I feel like a sponge out there just soaking it all in."

"So what was new this week?"

"This week we were dealing with issues related to migrant workers. They really are the backbone for many of the large producers, and with the current political climate there's a lot of fear about the future. We were brainstorming with a group of producers and others in the industry to plan contingencies for future changes."

"That sounds so interesting. I'm guessing it really requires you to be creative with your strategies and to get comfortable facing your clients' fears arm-in-arm with them."

"You are a very perceptive woman, Stella. Those were two of the biggest take-aways for me."

They finished breakfast and headed for the stables.

"Brandon, I would like to introduce you to Ranger. Ranger, this is Brandon." Ranger was the larger and more spirited of Stella's horses. He was a great roping Quarter horse that got bored and distracted at times. Stella found that if she took him out for a good hard run periodically, he was steadier in his work. Maybe they would open the throttle and get a run in today.

"Well Ranger, aren't you a handsome fella?" Brandon quickly made friends with Ranger. Stella pointed to the tack. Brandon saddled up and was ready to go in no time.

"This here is Molly. She's my all-around good girl."

"She's a beauty. I bet you two have fun together, don't you?"

"We do, indeed. She has quite the personality. It won't surprise me if she pulls a trick or two on us today. She knows this isn't a workday."

"It sure is a beautiful day for a ride." Brandon looked around the yard and the area surrounding.

"I guess I forget to notice because it's nice here almost all the time."

"I prefer this to the dust and smog trapped in

the city." Brandon paused and looked down. "I don't mean to be complaining. It's just that you notice the air quality when you're used to having this kind of purity."

"I noticed it too when I drove down to the airport and flew out. There's a layer of grime that hovers over the city. From the airplane, I looked down and wondered what it was doing to all those people and animals down there. It would not be my first choice as a place to live." Stella thought briefly about Jed and his wife, having to leave the pristine, open country up north and move to the city. "I guess sometimes our lives require us to be in those places."

"They do. For me, I get out of town every weekend and it won't be permanent."

"No? You don't think so?"

"Nope. I'm there to finish my education by practicing in the real world with some very experienced attorneys. Eventually, it would be ideal for me to set up a satellite office of this firm or branch out on my own and build a practice that will allow me to live outside the city. I've even thought of getting my pilot's license so I can travel to clients more efficiently."

"What a brilliant idea." Stella looked out on the horizon and pointed off to her right. "Let's head over that way. There are some cool old etchings in some boulders back in there.”

“Awesome. Glad I have my phone on me. Maybe I can grab some pictures.”

“Sure. Head for that outcropping there.” Stella pointed to the place. They guided the horses and started off with a trot, letting the horses warm up and Ranger get used to a new rider. Before long they were cantering to their destination. Stella held back from a full gallop; she wanted Ranger to be comfortable with Brandon first. Before they reached their destination, Molly ran up on Ranger and nudged his hind end with her head, causing him to move ahead faster. Brandon looked toward Stella and laughed. He lifted his cowboy hat and, with both arms raised over his head, rode off free with the wind.

They slowed as they approached the petroglyphs. Stella was not positive the rock carvings were authentic, but Martin assured her that an anthropology professor had authenticated them.

“Hey, Miss Molly! You are quite the tease, aren’t you?” Brandon dismounted and reached out to Molly.

“I knew she would have something up her sleeve. It’s a good thing Ranger is used to antics.

She might have spooked one of the other horses."

"I can't say I've ever had the experience before. She's a tease."

"She is. Follow me up this way. It's just a few minutes back up in these boulders. The horses will be fine." Stella wore hiking boots, expecting this climb. Unfortunately, she didn't forewarn Brandon. He had slick-soled cowboy boots on. He stopped at the top of the first boulder and tugged them off.

"What the heck are you doing down there?" Stella had passed behind another boulder and couldn't see him, but she could hear that he wasn't behind her.

"Just changing my footwear. Be right there." The boulders were smooth. Brandon tucked his socks in his boots and headed up the trail. He was quickly on Stella's tail.

"There you are." Stella looked down at Brandon's white feet sticking out from under his jeans. She laughed. "Sorry, I should have warned you we might climb some."

"Not to worry. I'm adaptable. The rock is already warming up, and it feels great." Stella watched Brandon climb around on the boulders. He was in excellent shape.

"Just another hundred feet up there and to

the left. I don't hear any water running so it's probably dry or there may be a small pool sitting up there. Just above that you can look up and see the carvings."

They climbed to the top where there was a ring of boulders that formed a bowl of pooled water. There were damselflies and other insects. Small lizards scattered as they moved closer.

"These are awesome!" Brandon pulled his phone out and started snapping pictures. "How old are they?"

"Martin says they're about eight hundred years old. There are some around that state that are thousands of years old."

"Any idea what they mean?"

"They are images from the daily life of the indigenous people. Like there." Stella pointed to an image. "Those two are frogs, but what their significance is I don't know. Those figures with their arms in the air are supposedly hunters. Beside them, there are animals with their feet in the air. Maybe it was a successful hunt." Brandon snapped photos of Stella pointing out the images. She wasn't a fan of having her picture taken, but she tossed her head and smiled, just for Brandon.

"That makes perfect sense. I hope you don't mind me taking your picture. This is a day I want stored in my memory for a long time. Besides, my mom will ask me how the day was."

Stella laughed. "Oh yeah. Could you forward those to me? I've got the same issue on my end. So, I had better get some photos of you, too." She raised her phone and snapped some photos too. She'll get some pictures of Brandon on Ranger as well. He looked good in the saddle.

They climbed up past the pool. About twenty minutes later, they were at the top of the ridge looking down over the valley.

"This sure is beautiful. We've got some places at our ranch that remind me of this. I think it's more dramatic here, though." Brandon's family ranch was about thirty miles south of Drake's ranch.

"How about we climb down and take a ride east along the fence line? It's just on the other side of that patch of trees there. If we follow that fence, we will eventually end up back at the ranch. The trees will shade us. I haven't seen the herd for a week. It'll be nice to just get a look at them."

"You are a herd nerd, Stella. Have you always been this crazy about cows?"

"Cows, horses, bulls, even a few goats. We always had chickens, but there was only one of them I got attached to. Dogs and barnyard cats are a given." Stella laughed. "I guess I am kind of nerdy, huh?"

"I'm teasing you. I love your passion for your job. I meet so many people in the legal profession that are miserable. Farmers and ranchers, not so much. They all are doing what they love. They aren't all getting rich but they wouldn't trade their work for a desk job, ever."

"That's how I feel and now, with this new position, I'm going even further off that corporate grid. Off any grid, really."

"Yeah. That will be different, living off the land like that. How are you feeling about that?"

Stella paused her downhill climb and turned to Brandon. "I'm so freaking excited I can hardly wait to get there!"

She smiled and twirled back around to go downhill.

"So Stella?" Brandon paused while she turned back around toward him. "Aren't you even a little concerned about being alone out in the canyon?"

"Honestly, no. I'm a good shot. I won't hesitate to take the head off a snake, even if it means I shoot a hole in my bedroll." They laughed.

"Really, I was thinking what if your horse went lame or threw you and you got hurt?"

"I got some great instruction from Jed about

which rides are okay to solo and which ones to always take a hand with me. I'll have the satellite phone as a backup."

"Not sure how much good that will do if a bobcat crosses your path but I admire your strength." Brandon understood the need to follow your dream. He was doing it. He knew from an early age that he had a journey to take away from the ranch, only to return to that way of life again one day. Once living on the range gets in your blood, it's hard to do anything else.

They finished their day with lunch from the kitchen refrigerator. Stella made sandwiches and tossed Brandon a bag of chips. They grabbed sodas and sat outside on the patio to eat. Clara and Martin had gone to church and to do their weekly shopping. Only two hands were around.

"I will miss this place a little." Stella spoke to the open space of the yard. "This has been a great place for me to grow up."

Brandon looked at her and tried to read her eyes. She was deep in thought. He gave her the space to just be. Her life was changing in a big way and, he hoped, for the better. They sat in silence for a few minutes.

Stella turned to Brandon. "Thanks for coming out today. It was nice of you to indulge my need to be in my space for the day."

"It was my pleasure, Stella. Thanks for showing me around and…" He raised his soda. "Making my lunch."

Stella laughed. "Oh, now that was my pleasure."

10

Moving to Watson took on a life of its own. It shocked Stella to learn all the steps it took to buy a house and move in. Co-ordinating all the inspections on the property, choosing a garage design and managing the required paperwork, on top of the work at Winding Slough Ranch and preparing for the transition to Rabbit Creek Ranch, took all her time and attention.

Brandon understood the demands on Stella, but was eager to move their budding relationship forward. He understood why there were no responses to his messages. He waited until Saturday evening, three weeks after their riding date, to call her. Stella answered, but was in no mood to talk.

"Hey, Brandon. So sorry I haven't been able to get back to you. Life has been so hectic for me. In fact, at this moment I'm loading up some supplies to take to the ranch up north and it's not a good time to talk."

The interruption irritated Stella and she let it show in her voice. It felt selfish of her to be dodging him; she wasn't sure this was the right time to fit a relationship in, yet she didn't walk away from what they had started. Her fears were consuming her. Fears of failure and being abandoned, the need to do everything perfectly and have all the answers, were interfering with the ability to read her own heart.

"Okay. I'm getting the feeling that it might be awhile until the right time comes. Tell you what Stella. I don't mean to be a pest and I really don't want to tarnish what I think has been a wonderful start to a relationship, so I will give you all the space and time you need to get settled and hope that when that happens you'll call me. Meanwhile, you know where to find me and if there's anything I can do for you, please let me know. You take care now."

Brandon wouldn't hang on the phone and negotiate for Stella's time and attention. He meant his words. He wanted to see her succeed, and right now that meant she had to fully commit to her transition. His heart was sad. He liked Stella a lot, but it wouldn't help her, or him, to get in her way right now.

***

STELLA SHOVED the rest of the supplies into the back of her pickup and loaded the horses in the trailer. Today was the day to take possession of her new home, and tomorrow she would be the new foreman of Rabbit Creek Ranch. She felt anger rise from deep in her belly as she worked. *"Of course, he would abandon me. That's what men do."* It was distorted thinking and she knew it, but now was not the time to talk herself down. She had to say her goodbyes and hit the road.

It was Sunday. The crew onsite, Clara, and Martin, gathered around her pickup and trailer. They shared hugs and well wishes. Clara dabbed the corners of her eyes. Martin swaddled Stella in a big, long bear hug. She would miss them all, but mostly Martin. He was her mentor.

Stella ran through her mental checklist several times during the two-hour drive to her new home. Clara had gathered together some basic supplies to get her started. She could clean and would have food for a few days before she would need to go to the store and stock up. For today, she planned to stop at Maxine's Diner, chat with Edna if she was working, and order some food to go.

"Well, if it isn't my friend Stella. Everyone!" she called out. "Please meet Watson's newest resident, Stella!" Edna was working and hadn't forgotten her new friend. The after-church crowd was just dissipating. Stella smiled and waved to the diners.

"Hello, Edna. Thanks for the introduction. How did you know I was moving in today?"

"Oh, honey. You have a lot to learn about Watson. First, I look outside and see that pickup of yours heaped to the brim with supplies and two horses tied to the trailer eating my grass."

"Your grass? Is this your place?"

Edna laughed. "Don't look so surprised. Yes, this is my place."

"Well then, who is Maxine?"

"That's a story for another time. We'll add it to the list. Here, let's get you a place to rest your weary self. You've been working really hard now, haven't you?"

"That's an understatement, and I just realized how hungry I am."

"Well, let Edna just fix you right up. Strawberry or chocolate?"

"What?"

"Do you prefer strawberry or chocolate?"

"Strawberry, I guess."

"Me too. I'll be back shortly. Drink this nice glass of ice water and close your eyes for a few minutes. I'll be back in a few."

Stella looked around the restaurant. Guests were greeting one another, and some stopped by her table to introduce themselves and inquire about her.

"Well hello, neighbor. I'm Sam Barton and this is my wife Deanna. We live out east a bit. Jed and his wife are friends of ours. We all grew up together around these parts. He gave us a heads-up to watch out for you. Said you're a talented cowboy moving up here to run the herd he's been managing. Sad thing about his wife, but hey, we're happy to meet you."

"It's so nice to meet you, too. Thanks for stopping by and introducing yourself. It'll be awhile before I remember everyone's names, I'm afraid."

"Here hun." Deanna smiled and handed Stella a napkin with names and cell phone numbers scribbled on it. "This should help, at least for now."

"This is perfect! I hope to see you around."

"You will. It's a small place and we all cross paths regularly here." Sam tipped his hat and put his arm around Deanna. "We're heading out now to play with the grandkids. Seriously, call us if you need anything. I hear you're moving into the old Porch place. That's about five miles from us. If you need help to load or move boxes, we can be there in no time."

"Thank you very much. I just might take you up on that offer. I'm not losing this napkin, for sure." Stella patted the napkin and smiled. She gave them a gentle wave as they walked away. *Mom will be so happy to hear I've already met some people. Seems like a nice place to be.*

"Here's that lunch I promised you." Edna set down a plate heaping with food - a huge grilled burger with the works and French fries. She handed Stella a large strawberry shake in a real glass and held out a matching shake as she slid into the booth. "Cheers to new beginnings."

Stella smiled. "You do not understand just how much is changing."

"Is that right? You leave a man behind on top of changing jobs and getting a new house?"

Stella looked at Edna and laughed. "Are you psychic, or what? You seem to know everything."

"Just about everything. That was just a lucky guess on my part."

"Well, it's not like I really had a man to leave but…" Stella shared the experience of her two dates with Brandon and his parting words from earlier in the day.

"Honestly babe, he sounds like a real gentleman. He's just giving you space, he's not running away, no matter what your brain says. I get it, I really do. I've been around and had just about every kind of failed relationship you can have. None of my guys would have been so considerate. They would push for what they wanted, not what was best for me. Don't write him off yet."

Stella held up her half-eaten burger. "This is the best doggone burger I've had in a long time. Grilled to perfection!"

"So, you will get set up in your new house today and let those horses loose in the pasture?"

"I had the prior owners and the realtor walk the fence and make sure it was safe to let the horses out. They assured me it was. As for setting up the house, not really. I should have a mattress delivered there today but other than that, I have made no decisions on furniture or paint, dishes or anything."

"That's fine. It will all come together. I've got some extra lawn chairs and a folding table you can use for now. I'm happy to bring them over later. We close early on Sundays. I'll grab a bottle of wine and two glasses, throw those things in the truck and head over. Got to give you the Watson welcome."

"Edna, you're so kind. Let's do it. I'm hoping the sellers cleaned the house up like they promised and I won't need to do a lot of that just to sleep and eat there for now."

"I'm sure it's fine. You enjoy your lunch. This is your one and only meal that's on the house. Consider it my welcome gift to you."

"That's not necessary."

"Of course it's not. It's a gift. Just say thanks, Stella."

"Thank you, Edna. I appreciate it a bunch."

"Good. Now, I've got to get these tables bussed and help get the kitchen cleaned up and prepped for tomorrow's breakfast. I'll be by about five and don't worry about something to eat. I've got a mess of ribs at my house that I need some help eating. I'll bring them out."

"You're the best! Thanks, Edna. See you later and again, thank you."

Edna waved her off as she rushed to clear the tables.

<hr>

Stella left a twenty-dollar tip - plenty to cover the food and thank Edna. She loaded the horses into the trailer and drove the twenty minutes home. It may have been longer, for she took her time, making a mental note of landmarks on the way. Driving out of town, the water tower stood tall on the right with its white face and bold green letters spelling out the name of the town. Three miles further, on the left, was the cemetery.

It surprised Stella to see vehicles in the yard when she arrived. Before she could get out of the pickup, the contractor building the garage was standing at the door to greet her.

"Well, you must be Stella." The tall, good-looking, muscular man in his late fifties held out a giant hand to shake. "I'm Jeff Kline, here to build your garage."

He nodded to Stella's right where the garage was being built.

"Nice to meet you in person. Thank you for all the phone calls, emails and texts over the past few weeks. Looks like you are buttoning it up. It looks great! Just what I wanted."

"That's right, ma'am. Got the boys out here just touching up the paint and hanging the cabinets inside. It's been a real pleasure working with you. You knew what you wanted, and that helped a bunch."

"Mind if I look inside? It's a little hard to envision from afar."

"Come on over, take a look and meet the guys."

Jeff toured her around the new building and introduced her to his two sons who were helping him. Stella complimented Jeff on the perfect match in paint color and roof pitch as the house. The shop and tack areas in the garage had built-in cabinets and closets and were well organized for Stella's use.

"Perfect. It's all just perfect."

"Thank you, ma'am. I hope you don't mind, but I did a walk-through of the house with my niece and her husband. There were a few little things I tightened up. Would you mind if we took a walk over there and I can show you?"

Stella nodded. As they walked to the house, she noticed that someone had cleaned up the landscape and swept the front porch. Jeff pulled a key from his pocket and opened the front door. He handed her the key and held the door open for her to enter.

"It looks so fresh and clean in here. I didn't realize the paint was so fresh. When you see a house only once you don't catch all the details."

"Well, actually ma'am, we came over and helped the kids freshen up the place. After they pulled their pictures and things off the walls, we patched 'em up and gave them a little paint. I sure hope you like it."

They walked through the house. Jeff pointed out where he had tightened cabinet knobs, replaced some cracked electrical outlet covers and made the place move-in ready for Stella.

"You really have an attention to detail, don't you? It looks fantastic and I'm so grateful to have such a clean place to move into." As she said this, a box truck drove up to the house. "That must be my new mattress. Excuse me while I get this delivery."

Stella met the driver at the front door. He offered to bring the large box into the house and Jeff was eager to help. They put the mattress in the master bedroom.

"Thank you, gentlemen! I appreciate your help." Stella would usually be offended that the men assumed she couldn't wrangle a large heavy box a few dozen feet, but not today. Today she was happy to have all the help she could get. She was tired, disoriented, and had a lot to do before she could rest for the night.

Jeff and his boys wrapped up their work. They helped Stella unload the pickup and trailer. She pastured the horses, who stayed close to the house. Jeff was talking with Stella on the front porch when Edna drove up.

"Well, if it isn't Edna Holt!" Jeff tipped his baseball cap to Edna as she got out and walked to the back of her truck.

"Jeff Kline, as I live and breathe! How are you doing?" Edna could look at Jeff all day. He was perfect - a hot body, handsome, successful, and an all-around good guy.

Jeff walked around to the back of Edna's truck. "Can I help you with something?"

"You sure can." Edna looked at Stella and winked. "I have a table and two chairs for this little lady here. We can't have her eating off the floor, clean as it might be."

"Here, here, let me take those things in." Jeff grabbed the table and chairs like they had no weight or bulk at all. Edna reached into the cab of the truck and pulled out two reusable grocery bags. Stella reached out to take one of them.

"Here's a little dinner. How are you doing?"

"Great. What's up with you and Jeff?"

"Unrequited love I'm afraid."

"Are you sure? I saw the way he rushed up to help you. Is he single?"

"Yes, he's a widower. I have flirted until I was blue in the face with that man and he's never let on that he was sweet on me. Guess he knows my reputation for wanting only the bad boys."

11

———————

Stella launched right into her new job. Jed spent the first two days with her before releasing her to manage the herd. He invited four hired hands that he trusted. He introduced them to Stella, who shared some of her background. She felt comfortable with each of them and was happy to have tried-and-true hands to choose from for the first drive to rotate pastures coming up in three weeks. Until then she would repair the fence, set minerals and salt in the pasture, and do a host of other activities that keep the ranch running.

At the end of the first week, Stella packed her bedroll and a modest supply of rations. She and Ranger headed to the lower canyon near the new pasture. This was a trial run, a test, a chance to harden herself to sleeping under the stars with the scorpions and snakes. She tried not to dwell on the creatures she shared the wilds with, but sent a general prayer for protection out into the world as she drank in the beauty of the area.

On the first evening, she straddled a small boulder eating instant noodles heated with water from a thermos. She inhaled the fresh scent of the pines and watched as the pale blue sky transformed into a colorful masterpiece with strokes of peach, violet, vibrant orange, burning yellow and red. Stella had seen the sunset a thousand times, but it was never as brilliant as it was tonight. She was prepared to lie under the stars, listen to the coyotes in the distance and embrace this new life, with fewer walls.

Two evenings later, Stella returned to her new home with a renewed joy for life. She was not unhappy before, but she did not know she could be this thrilled. The sky was bluer, the trees greener, and her satisfaction with life greater. Her home was bare but she didn't notice. She saw the closet where her clothes could now hang out of sight, a full-sized refrigerator she could fill with as many pitchers of water and tea as she wanted for those hot days under the Arizona sun when it seemed impossible to quench her thirst.

For days, and then weeks, Stella thought of nothing other than her new herd, Watson and setting up house. The weekend after her maiden voyage on the trail, she awakened to a country tune playing on her telephone. It was five in the morning on a Sunday, a day she had intended to take for leisure.

"Good morning, Mom. What's up?"

"What do you mean, what's up? I haven't heard from you for two weeks. I was just worried about you, that's all."

Stella sat up in bed, brushed her hair away from her face and wiped her eyes. "Oh Mom, I'm sorry. There's nothing to worry about. I'm wonderful!"

"You can't blame a mom for worrying. You know, I worry about you being alone up there, in the wilds."

"First, Mom, you'll be happy to know I'm resting in my comfortable bed in my very own house. It's cozy in here. The only thing missing is a dog. I need a good herding dog." The thought just dawned on her. It would be nice to have a canine companion.

"Well, that sounds sweet. Last time we talked

you were planning to spend some time in the canyon and then I never heard from you again."

"Oh Mom, I'm sorry. I turned my phone off when I went out there. There wouldn't be any service anyway but I took the satellite phone in case I needed it. I didn't. Anyway, I so enjoyed the silence that I totally forgot about turning my phone back on for days after returning. It was magical!"

"Who is this and where is my little Stella? This sounds like someone who has found their new happy place."

Stella laughed. "You couldn't be more right, Mom. I am thrilled to be here. I've always pre-ferred being outdoors. Now, I live with nature more intimately. And my house! MY house, did you hear that? MY house is perfect. It doesn't need me to be here to water it and feed it and keep the rain out of the living room. It just needs me to visit sometimes and laugh and enjoy the sunshine coming in the windows."

"Seriously Stella, are you taking drugs? I've never heard you so happy."

"You're funny, Mom. That's the thing, not that I would ever take them but I don't need drugs. I have found my bliss." Stella took a deep breath. She wasn't sure she was ready for a break in her solitary space but she knew it would be good for both of them. "Are you ready to come visit? I mean not for a few weeks, but we could start planning."

"Of course I am! I thought you would never ask. I'm ready whenever you are. I could drive out if there's anything you want me to bring from the house. You can have any of your bedroom furniture. I have some other things…"

"There's no need for you to drive out. I can get whatever I need by going into Parsonville or into the city if I need to. There is a consignment place in Watson too, that I'm told might have some décor. Besides, I can get anything I want by ordering online."

"That's true enough. Just the other day we got a second smoker delivered. I bought it online and it was here in two days. Your dad will smoke some of the salmon he caught in Alaska. I'll freeze some and bring it to you."

"That sounds like a real treat. Hold on a second while I get myself out of bed and go look at my calendar." Stella rolled out of the mattress, still on the floor awaiting her decision on a bed frame. She flipped on lights as she walked out to the kitchen island. A Watson Hardware Store calendar lay there with notes already occupying some squares. "Okay, you there?"

"Yep, I'm here with my calendar and a pen."

"Great. I've got a trail-riding coming up. I think if we look three weeks out, it should work great. I will have work to do but will come home in the evening on those days. How does that sound?"

"Perfect. I have about a week there without appointments or meetings. Does that sound okay? A week?"

"Wonderful. We can do a lot of damage to my bank account in a week and bring some personality into my little abode."

They finalized the plans, caught up on Buffalo Ridge gossip and said their goodbyes. Stella made herself coffee in a new coffeepot, another package delivered to her front door. The contradictions of the happiness under the stars and the happiness felt surrounded by shiny new things delivered in cardboard boxes did not escape her. She shrugged it off as being human in a complex world.

Stella sat in silence with her coffee, looking out the window toward the pasture where Ranger and Molly grazed. They seemed content in their new home, and Ranger was a star at navigating the trail. He was surefooted and calm.

She reflected on the conversation with her mother. Yvette asked about Brandon. Stella simply told her mother that she had been so busy she hadn't seen Brandon. Truth was, with great effort Stella had pushed Brandon from her mind since she arrived in Watson. Except when she was alone at Rabbit Creek when all barriers dissolved. She thought about their last date, climbing the boulders and riding at the ranch.

Stella enjoyed that day and Brandon seemed to also. But Stella knew she didn't have time to commit to a relationship right now and it wouldn't be fair to Brandon to pretend that she did. *"We could still be friends, couldn't we?"* she thought.

She drafted a text message to Brandon. *Getting settled and loving it. Hope all is well with you.* It was too early to send; she would send it later in the day.

EDNA CAME by later in the day to catch up. She brought leftovers to share with Stella, who still hadn't equipped her kitchen. She was waiting for Yvette to help with that. She had never had her own kitchen before.

"So, guess who came into the restaurant this week?"

"I don't know. The governor?"

Edna laughed. "Even better. Jeff Kline."

"He's such a great guy. So, what did he have?"

"Seriously? You want to know what he ordered?"

"Well, what else happened? Did he ask you out or something?"

"In fact he did, smarty-pants!"

"Well, did you say yes?" Stella laughed to see her new friend so giddy over a guy.

"Of course I did!" Edna blushed.

"And, when is this date going to happen?"

"As a matter of fact, it's next Saturday. He has a cowboy singer friend putting on a little fundraising performance for a local family. We will go to dinner and then to hear his friend. I even agreed to donate a gift certificate to their silent auction."

"Way to go Edna!" Stella held her hand up for a high-five.

"Maybe you should go, too. It might be good to mingle with the locals… Besides, I might need a distraction if Mr. Wonderful proves to be boring."

"First, I highly doubt he will be boring. Second, I will be heading out on the ranch next week and won't be around."

"I thought maybe you were ready to invite

that lawyer fella up and make up for running off?"

"Brandon? I didn't run off... Oh, shoot. Hold on a minute." Stella picked up her phone and pressed send on the message she drafted early that morning. "I'm so, so happy here. Just me, my house, my horses, my new job and..." She tapped her friend's arm. "My new friend. I'm not ready for more, just yet. Besides, my mom is coming up to see me in a few weeks. I'll have plenty of entertainment for a while."

"Sweet. I bet she's excited."

"More than! She can't wait to get her hands on this place and get it furnished and decorated. She's a wiz that way. I'm sure she'll be cooking up a storm and filling my freezer too. I'm looking forward to it. I'll be sure you get to meet her."

"I bet she's a hoot. Be sure and bring her by the diner, if nothing else."

"I will. She'll love it. Anyway, let's get back to Mr. Wonderful. Is this a blue jeans event?"

"It had better be. That's all I've got. I thought I would find something more conservative in my closet for a shirt. Maybe something even a little western looking. You know me, I tend to flaunt the girls a little." Edna motioned toward her well-endowed chest, the cleavage peeking out of the low v-neck t-shirt.

Stella laughed. "If you've got them, flaunt them. That saying was always lost on my mini breasts but I don't care. Riding is easier like this."

"You're right there. I used to ride, but now I'll only do it for the right guy. Those are double sports bra days for me and that can get mighty warm." They laughed. Stella loved having a female friend she could talk about girly stuff with. It had been a long time since she had that outlet.

Stella's phone chimed with a new text message. *Nice to hear from you. Glad it's going well. Tied up in TX on a huge case.*

"Well, it looks like Brandon's not pining over me. He's just as busy as I am. He's working on a case in Texas."

"Oh, Texas - where everything's bigger. Never been."

"Well, the state is big, women's hair is big, and that's all I know about Texas. I've been to some rodeos down there and picked up some livestock with my dad when I was in high school." Stella took a bite of the chicken and biscuits Edna brought. "This is fantastic. Maybe someday you can show me a little something in the kitchen. I'm rusty."

"Sure thing. I love creating in the kitchen. That's how my interest in the diner started. Maxine was my mother's aunt. I came up here to live with her after I got in a little trouble down south. She saved me from ruining my life. As she got older and started getting sick, I took over more and more of her duties at the diner and she eventually deeded it to me. I'm really blessed to have such a big break in what could have been a disaster of a life."

Edna poured them each a glass of wine and raised her glass. Stella raised hers in unity. "To second chances."

12

Stella marveled at the desert-friendly cattle. Slightly smaller than the beef cattle her family raised at Buffalo Ridge Ranch, these cattle tolerated heat better, ate a wider variety of plants native to the high desert and were in constant motion, unlike the Plains cattle who could stand still and eat from the same patch of grass. In the high desert, the cattle chased their food from scanty patch to scanty patch.

"These cattle are amazing in the way they have adapted to this environment, aren't they?" Stella started the campfire to heat dinner for herself and the hired hand, Matt.

"To be honest ma'am, this is the only cattle work I've ever done but I've heard that cattle in other parts would never eat the craggy shrubs and cactus these cows eat." Matt had worked on the ranch with Jed for several years. He originally came along with a hard-luck story, and Jed took him under his wing. Matt proved to be a hard worker, and when he wasn't working for Rabbit Creek Ranch he was working construction or handyman jobs to support his young family.

"Where I come from in South Dakota, the cattle like their green grass, hay, and feed and they'd like it on a silver platter, if you don't mind." Matt chuckled with Stella. "It's not just the feed, either. These cattle here live on little water. They also seem calmer and can climb these rocks like mountain goats."

"That's right. The most challenging part of this job is finding some of these cows that get deep in the rocks. They're hard to get to sometimes. I bet there's another thing you don't know about these cows."

Stella looked to Matt and smiled, her eyebrows raised, waiting for Matt to wow her with his knowledge as she stirred their dinner for the last night sleeping under the stars. They had moved the herd to their new grazing land and doctored a half-dozen with small injuries along the way. "Well, two things. First, their meat tastes different. My wife says it tastes like the cows have been eating flowers. I think it tastes like berries and sage."

"That's interesting. I don't know that I've ever tried it. Thanks for that info. I'm putting that on my list of things to try. What's the other thing you know about these cows?"

"They calve easily and don't get sick."

"Matt, this is all great news. Thanks for agreeing to take this ride with me. It's a little unusual to be working for a woman out here like this, but I hope I didn't cause you any heartache."

"No, ma'am. It was just like working with Jed. Silent and efficient. That works well for me. Your food may be a little better than his, but I would never complain." Matt looked at Stella while talking, sincerity in his message.

"Thanks, Matt, and will you please thank your wife for sending brownies along. That was a treat, and I enjoyed them. I hope I can meet her and your kids someday."

"She would like that, too. She grew up on a ranch and it excited her to learn the new foreman out here was a lady. She's progressive like that, too. She's a great mom to our kids and a super teacher, too. God blessed me on the day I met her, that's for certain." Matt picked a blade of the dry grass standing nearby and tossed it into the fire as he spoke.

The next morning they skipped breakfast and rode to their pickups and trailers with the first light. Matt got home in time to go to the late church service with his family. Stella put Ranger out to pasture and unloaded her gear. She took a long hot shower before cleaning and storing the tack and equipment.

She sat down at her computer and drafted an email to Martin, summarizing the details of the move and condition of the cattle. With a smile on her face, she wrote her conclusion. "All in all I would call this a successful maiden voyage. Matt was a superior hand, and the cattle were all well-mannered."

Before she could locate and unplug her phone, she had a text from Martin.

We knew you were the right cowboy for the job. Congratulations on your first of many successful moves. Now, take a couple of days off.

Stella smiled at the screen. She would respond later. For now, she could feel the hunger rising in her stomach. She grabbed her keys and wallet and headed to Maxine's for a late breakfast.

"Well, if it isn't Stella!" Edna greeted Stella at the door with a one-arm hug as she passed by to refill coffee cups. "Grab any seat, hun, and I'll be with you momentarily."

Stella smiled at her friend and nodded to the handful of customers lingering from the after-church crowd.

"Good to see you in from the canyon. Tell me all about it after I get your order in. What are you having today?" Edna sat across from Stella, looking pretty with her hair curled and lipstick on.

"My, don't you look nice today!"

"You think so? Thanks. What'll you have and then we need to chat." Edna winked at Stella as she stood to encourage Stella to decide what she wanted faster. Stella ordered. Edna returned with two cups and a coffee pot.

"How was the…" Stella didn't finish her sentence before Edna jumped in.

"Mr. Wonderful is all that. The first date…"

"Wait. What do you mean by the FIRST date?" Stella wiggled in the booth and leaned into the table to listen closely.

"That's right. There's been more than one. Stella, I don't know why I wasted so much of my life chasing the bad boys. Jeff is perfectly wonderful and a real gentleman."

"Can you back it up just a little? Tell me about the fundraiser."

"Yeah, yeah. I wish you could have been there. It was a huge event. Several of the towns around here donated things and people came from all around. The music was great, and the company was even better."

"Oh, Edna, I'm so happy for you. Everything happens in its own time. Maybe I'm your good luck charm."

"That's it! You are! I'm glad you're back. We need a girls' night to catch up. How about you come over to my place this evening?"

"I would love to. Boss told me to take a couple of days off so I can even sleep in tomorrow morning. What shall I bring?"

"Honey, you've been out with the cows for a week. I'll just be glad if you come with your sunny disposition, and your eyes open. I'll be home around five so come any time after."

"Sounds terrific."

"Have you heard from Brandon at all?"

Stella pulled her cell phone out of her pocket. "I haven't even checked my messages yet. I showered and came in here for something to eat. I'll let you know later if there's any update. I don't expect to hear from him. The ball's really in my court."

"True. Let me grab your breakfast." Edna hustled off to make Stella's toast and grab her potatoes and eggs with a side of bacon. Stella never tired of this meal.

LATER, Stella walked around her property, checking fences and gates. When her mother came, she would enlist her help in beautifying the yard. She wanted to plant flowers but had not decided where or what flowers. Landscaping was missing throughout the property. With some tender loving care and her mother's advice, the yard would be looking homey in no time.

Stella slid her laptop out of the kitchen cupboard to browse furniture ideas for the house. She paused first to check for text messages. Her mom and two brothers had written just to say hi. Stella quickly responded so they knew she was alive and well and back home. There were no messages from Brandon. She wondered if he was still in Texas. She sent him a message, to test the waters. *Still in TX? How's the case going?*

As Stella browsed through websites looking at dining table sets, her mind wandered back to Brandon. She realized she did not know what his apartment looked like in the city or what he would look for in a home. Perhaps they stayed in hotels, or maybe they had corporate condos when they traveled to Texas. She looked up McGraw and Lipson. It seemed to be a huge law firm, so they probably had permanent housing for partners and associates traveling back and forth.

Stella turned to Internet pages of living room furniture for small homes. Furniture in earth tones and leather caught her fancy. She didn't trust herself to pick something of good quality that she might get bored with, even if she spent a lot of time away. Stella closed the computer and looked around for something to do. Back at Winding Slough, she read trade magazines Martin gave her or pulled a book from the library in the bunkhouse. She added books to her list of things to shop for.

Stella was walking to her pickup, planning to take it to town and run it through the carwash, when her phone rang. It was Brandon.

"Hey, Brandon!"

"Hello, Stella! How are you doing? Did I get you at a bad time?"

"No, this is a perfect time. I just got in from a week on the trail and going through a little withdrawal, actually. How are you? Are you still working down in Texas?"

"I'm back in the city. Our first mediation attempt didn't go well, so now we will spend the next several months getting ready for trial. I'll be spending most of my time in Texas, so I guess you're not the only one with a timing problem."

"Thanks for saying that, Brandon. I feel like I sort of crowded you out hastily. I was so excited about my new job and my work."

"I didn't feel like that, at all. I mean I really enjoyed spending time with you and would like to do more of that, but I'm also a realist. We are both young in our careers and sometimes that just has to be the priority until we get established."

"That makes sense Brandon."

"I'm glad you reached out. There's something else I need to talk to you about. I think you know I'm meeting Martin to learn about his style of cattle operation. I have a lot to learn from him and other operators. When I talked to him last week, he suggested I interview you about the unique aspects of the Rabbit Creek Ranch operation."

"He did, did he? I've only been here for about a month and just finished my first cattle drive at Rabbit Creek. I know some things, but not everything."

Stella could hear the smile in Brandon's

voice. "Martin said you would say that. He said he was inviting you down to Winding Slough so I could interview the two of you together. Maybe he's already talked to you about that."

"He invited me to the ranch. I didn't know there was a meeting with you. I'll do my best to tell you what I've observed, what I learned by researching and what I feel in my gut as I look at the business."

"Thanks, Stella. I'll send you a list of the areas I've identified as places for me to learn more, but you may have other ideas to share."

"Sounds good. I'll do my homework and see you in a couple of weeks."

"Be well, Stella. I'm right here if you have questions about this. I appreciate you doing this."

Stella hung up and drove to Edna's house. Brandon's call unsettled her. It was nice to hear his voice and clear the air around the status of their relationship. Something needled at her about his motives for the information he sought from Martin and herself. She would talk with Martin about it later. For now, she was taking time off.

Edna was on the phone when Stella arrived at half-past five. Jeff was asking her to join him the following weekend for a family gathering.

Edna agreed to go. She brought a plate of cheese and crackers to the patio table with a glass of sangria for each of them. "I've got some stuffed potatoes for dinner. I hope you don't mind a meatless dinner. Some days I just can't take any more meat."

"That sounds good to me. I've been eating rations and smoky campfire food for a week so anything's a treat to me." Stella thanked Edna for the refreshing drink and studied her friend, waiting for her to share. "So, are you going to make me ask? Where's he taking you now?"

"He invited me to his son's birthday party next weekend. I'm not sure I'm ready to meet his family. I mean, I already know his family but to meet them this way means we're dating, right?"

Stella laughed. "Yeah, it would seem so. Maybe you should talk to Jeff about that. See what it means to him. He seems like a straight shooter and if he's taking you, you're his girl."

"That's what I thought, too. Stella, this seems surreal to me. No man has ever treated me as kindly as Jeff does and there is no, and I mean absolutely no, pressure from him."

"I'm guessing you didn't find him boring either or you wouldn't still be seeing him."

"No way! There is not a boring bone in his hunky body. He is well read, has traveled a lot, has grandchildren, knows every family for five hundred miles it seems, and can name every peak in that mountain range over there." Edna pointed to the west.

"What more could you ask for, Edna? Have you cooked him dinner yet, I mean here at home?"

"No, but that's on my short list of things to do. There just hasn't been time yet. We only see each other once a week, unless he stops in the diner. We're both busy with our work. Speaking of work, did you find out anything about Brandon's case? Is he still in Texas?"

"He's back in Arizona. I just talked with him before I came over. We had a nice chat. He sort of said the same thing about both being busy right now. No hard feelings from him. I'm going to see him in two weeks at a meeting with Martin. It will be all business but it will be good to see him again." Stella shifted in her chair. The uneasy feeling stayed with her, and she couldn't really name it.

"Anyway, I had a beautiful time last week and can't wait to go back to work in the canyon with the cattle again. I have two days off. My mom is coming to help me with my house, my brother Jesse wants to come for a visit, and I am getting a dog."

Edna laughed. "You will forget the guy and get a dog? You're heading down a path of perpetual single life with no return."

"Do you think men and dogs are mutually exclusive? I might just be buying myself some time to lick my wounds and regroup. Besides, I could use a good cow dog to help with the herd."

"Naw. I'm just teasing. I like your plan. Just shelve Brandon for now. If he's meant to come around, he will. Meanwhile, let's find a good dog. The Melchers have cattle dogs. Maybe they have a new litter on board. Muffy comes in for coffee with the ladies in the morning. I'll ask her."

"Muffy Melcher? Seriously? Now that would be a good reason not to get married right there."

"Listen, her maiden name wasn't any kinder to her. She's a beautiful woman, but who can say 'Muffy Topper' with a straight face."

Stella laughed loudly. "Oh, that poor girl. Yes, please ask Ms. Muffy about her puppies for me. Where's the nearest pound? I might take a ride there to look, too."

"That's about an hour and a half away. They have a website that shows the dogs they have in the shelter. It would be good for you to look there before you drive over. Now, how about some dinner?"

13

Yvette's visit was timely and productive. Together, Stella and her mom furnished and decorated Stella's new home with a clean, contemporary look dotted with rustic and animal print accents. All the essentials were put in place, the kitchen outfitted and organized. Yvette ironed and hung curtains on the last day there before heading to the airport.

"Stella, I think this place is ready to showcase on a home remodel television show. Can you believe we got all that done in a week?"

"After looking at my bank account, yes, I believe it." Stella smiled at her mom. Yvette was generous and made several purchases herself. "A

gift for your new home," she repeatedly explained.

"I hope Dad doesn't mind you giving me all
these gifts." Stella wouldn't allow herself to be
treated any differently than her siblings. Her
mother reassured her that Dan was on board
and the boys got their gifts in different ways and
in equal amounts.

"Stella, did Jesse say anything to you about
coming for a visit?" Yvette had been waiting for
Stella to raise the subject. Now that it was time
to leave, Yvette needed to bring it up.

"Yes, he did. He is settling the dates and then
he'll tell me when he's coming. That'll give me
more time under my belt to settle in with the
herd. Maybe I'll put him to work for a bit."
Stella turned to see Gus standing at the door.

"Come on in here, boy." She opened the
door for her new dog to come in. "Gus knows
these cattle from his puppy days. He will be a
great partner out in the canyon. He was Jed's
sidekick when he was running the ranch."

When she started looking for a new companion, Stella called Jed to see if he knew of any
pups around that were looking for homes. Jed
explained that his wife continued to be ill. She
was in and out of the hospital and rehab. They
were looking to re-home their dog. Gus was not

doing well in the city; with Jed spending days at the hospital, Gus wasn't getting the attention he deserved. Stella collected Gus from Jed's just after she picked up her mom from the airport. Stella and Gus were inseparable. Stella was eager to take him on their first trail ride together the following week. They would be out for only two nights checking the cattle, but that would be enough to see his demeanor with the cattle.

Yvette fell in love with Edna. She and Stella had to have their last meal together at the diner before driving into the city for Yvette's evening flight back to South Dakota.

"That Edna. She's the sun on a cloudy day, isn't she? I mean, she could make even the crabby ladies in the coffee club laugh." Yvette rinsed and dried a pot from the new cookware collection that arrived on the doorstep that morning. "She had me in stitches telling about her awkward teenage years and some trouble she got in. Thank God her mother had the foresight to remove her from the bad influences."

"It's been fun getting to know her. I was so blessed that first day I met her when I came up house hunting. She passes no judgment, just en-couragement." Stella took the pot from her mom and put it away in the cupboard next to the stove. She smiled. "It's so nice to have a fully furnished home of my own. I didn't know what a good feeling this could be. Don't get me wrong; I'm not ready to cash in my day job to stay at home. But we have created a sanctuary for me to retreat into after long days and nights on the trail."

Stella reached down to scratch Gus behind the ears. "And it seems like my new buddy here likes his bed, too."

"Well, I think that's it. Let me grab my bag and we can go grab some lunch." Yvette stopped beside her daughter as she passed by. She faced her and enveloped her in a warm embrace. She pulled back and smiled into her daughter's eyes. "I love you so much, my little sweet pea. Your dad and I are so proud of you. You are the most brave and creative woman we know and I am over the moon in love with the life you're creating for yourself. And wow, do I feel especially grateful to have two visits so closely together with you. I hope it's not so long until the next one."

"You can come visit any time now that I have my own place. Dad too. It was just so awkward to have visitors at the ranch, with no rooms to spare."

"We understood. I can see that this job will have you tied up so it'll be on us to travel more."

"And I have a spare room to boot! Here, let me grab that bag for you."

"Gus, you're going to stay home and keep an eye on things, okay? Go find your bed." Gus turned around and walked to his bed, in the living room by the fireplace where he had a wide view of the living room and a sky view through the huge window nearby.

"WELL, if it isn't the Bobbsey twins, or is it Thing One and Thing Two? I get mixed up sometimes." Edna reached out and pulled them both into a hug. "You gals pick your table. I've got a handsome contractor to say goodbye to and then I'll be right with you."

Stella and Yvette both smiled and raised their eyebrows at the flirty Edna. They settled into a booth where they both had a great view of Edna. She was packing a care package for Jeff, who looked like he was going back to work. He thanked her, put his hand on her arm and said something quietly that made her giggle like a schoolgirl. He dropped money on the counter, looked toward Stella and Yvette, tipped his baseball cap and left the diner.

"He sure is a big, handsome man, isn't he?"

Yvette's eyes followed Jeff out the door and to his pickup.

"He is, and his two sons that helped build my garage are a replica of him, only younger." It surprised Stella to see how closely the three men resembled each other with their baseball caps off.

"Is that right? Stella, did you ever…"

"I'm going to stop you right there, Mom. The boys are barely out of high school. One might still be in school. I don't need a match-maker. Remember how you said you were so proud of me? Well, I got here on my own and I like it this way. I'll let you know if the right guy comes around, but meanwhile you will have to be just as patient as I am." Stella patted her mom's hand.

"Well, you will see that lawyer friend next week. Maybe there are still some sparks there."

"Mom!" Stella exhaled in a loud rush as color rose in her cheeks. "I told you; anything that might happen between us is sitting on a back burner while we both grow in our careers. He's a nice guy, interesting and funny… "

"And handsome. I've seen his picture, remember."

"Okay, right, and handsome. But we're on ice right now."

"Well then, maybe someone else will come along. But when you see him next week, you'll be nice, right?"

"I will! I told you, we are still talking, but we're both realistic about what's possible right now. Anyway, I'm seeing him for business and my boss will be there."

"Business? What do you need a lawyer for?"

"He's just gathering information. I think his firm does work with lobbyists and they certainly represent a lot of big cattle producers across the country. He says he's informing himself about the different styles of cattle operations so he, and the firm, can have a full picture of the innovations currently in play and make recommendations for future laws."

"Who knew that they could build an entire law career around our little businesses?"

"You know Mom, some of these businesses are not that little. I don't think Buffalo Ridge Ranch is all that small. Maybe it was when you first started out, but it's no small thing now that you have the rodeo livestock and the larger herds."

"You're right. I've just never seen it as something to compare to the cattle barons of times past. Oh, good! Looks like Edna can join us now."

"Hello, my little chickadoodledees. How are you today? Ready to go to the airport Vette?" Edna scooted onto the seat beside Yvette. "I got a little bug this morning and made up some cute individual chicken pot pies. Just sent one home with Jeff for his dinner. Would you ladies like to try one? They have an exceptionally flaky crust, if I say so myself."

Edna squared her shoulders in mock pride, exaggerated the lengthening of her neck. She then collapsed her posture and smiled. "Of course, we have all the other usuals if you'd rather."

"I, for one, will have the pot pie. It sounds delightful." Yvette loved good home cooking. She had often toyed with writing a cookbook with a western flair, but never found the time.

"And for you miss Stella? A burger and a shake or…" Edna slid out of the booth to put their order in.

"I will have the pot pie too, if you have enough."

"I do. I'll bring some waters and, coffee for you both?" Edna left quickly with the orders and returned a few minutes later with a pot pie for each of them and coffee for all three.

They chatted while Yvette and Stella enjoyed their lunch. Yvette guessed the herbs and spices used as she devoured the entire pie. "You have just got to share your recipe with me. This is the best chicken pot pie I have ever eaten!"

"If you don't mind a recipe that measures by the dump and pour method, then I am happy to share with you. I'm so glad you enjoyed it."

The meal excited Stella. She was trying to think of a way to make it packable for the trail, but quickly became overwhelmed by the effort required to preserve the crust from getting soggy.

"So, Stella, you've got a big week coming up, is that right?" Edna winked at Stella, whose mouth was too full to protest. "Isn't this the week you see Brandon again? It's been how long now? Two months?"

Stella swallowed hard. "Now that's enough, Edna. I just told Mom, Brandon and I are on ice. Let's all just cool it now. And yes, I do have a big week. I'm heading out to the northwest quadrant tomorrow to check cows. This will be my first ride with Gus and I'm looking forward to it. I'll be out two nights and then I head down to Winding Slough."

"I'm saving my dance card for you for next Sunday. I want a blow-by-blow action packed report of this so-called meeting you're going to with Brandon. I think it's a ploy just to see you again."

"No, I don't think Martin would let that happen. Anyway, it's all business and I doubt I will see Brandon after that for months. He's working on that big case in Texas." Stella pushed the last bits of chicken pie filling around in the bowl. She had lost her appetite with all this talk of Brandon. She already had butterflies in anticipation of their meeting.

"Well, whatever happens, I'm sure you'll knock their socks off with your ideas for the ranch." Yvette and Stella had many talks during the week about the unique nature of ranching in the high desert. They drew some parallels with ranching in the Badlands, a much less rugged and harsh environment, but challenging.

"Thanks Mom. I'll let you know how it goes."

14

Stella drove into Winding Slough Ranch with excitement stirring her belly and a wave of nostalgia tugging at her heart. This ranch had been her playground to grow up in. Here, she polished her cowboy skills and built her confidence. She stepped out of the pickup feeling a foot taller than the day she first arrived six years ago.

"There's our beautiful Stella. It's so good to see you!" Clara rushed to greet Stella with a big hug. Martin was close behind. "Come in and have a cup of coffee. Brandon just called. Will be a half-hour late. Come! Come! I've got some blueberry coffeecake too."

"Clara, honey, can you serve that in my office? I will visit with Stella first, since we have some time before Brandon comes."

"Yes, yes, of course. I'll meet you both in there shortly."

Stella strolled with Martin to his office.

"How was your visit with your mom last week?" Martin motioned for Stella to sit in a tall leather chair in the parlor area of his office.

"It was fantastic! It would amaze you to see all we accomplished, and I still managed my work at Rabbit Creek."

Martin laughed gently at Stella. "Of course you did. You are not short on good mid-west work ethics, that's for sure. So, what did you get done at your house?"

"Everything! I mean it's furnished, decorated and I have a fully functioning kitchen."

Clara rushed into the office carrying a tray of coffee and coffee cake. "How on earth did you manage all that?"

"My mom is a planner. She had already picked out several options for me to choose from for furniture, and once I decided on the furniture, the rest fell into place. She wasn't at my house twenty-four hours and we had ordered almost all the furniture, rugs, bedding and bathroom essentials."

"She knows how to get it done. I must hire her the next time I'm updating a room."

"Oh, honey, you don't need any help spending money. You do just fine on your own." Martin looked to his wife and smiled.

"Now listen, Stella. I'm not sure exactly why Brandon is looking for all this information, but you can tell him whatever you want. He acted like he needed it right away. I don't know if that's because he has to go back to Texas or what. I trust him, so I'm not worried about his intent but it seems that there is a purpose other than general knowledge."

"Thanks for the heads-up Martin. It seemed a little odd to me too, that he couldn't just ask questions by email or wait until I had a little more experience under my belt. I'll do my best to bring factual information forward." Stella pulled out a dog-eared notebook. "I've been crunching some numbers and doing some research."

"I would expect nothing less from you, Stella. It looks like Brandon's coming up the drive now."

Brandon pulled into the yard and parked. Clara walked outside to greet him and escort him into the study.

"Here we are with some of my favorite people." Brandon shook Martin's hand. "It's nice to see you again, Martin. Thank you for making the time to see me."

Martin put his free hand on Brandon's shoulder. "Of course, son. It's always good to see you. I hope some good comes from all this information you're gathering."

A broad grin grew on Brandon's face. "I assure you, sir, it will."

Brandon moved in to hug Stella. "Stella, it's very nice to see you again. I hope it wasn't too much of an inconvenience for you to meet here at the ranch. I trust everything is going well up at Rabbit Creek. I hope to see the place one day."

"No, it was no problem. I wanted to come down and check in with Martin and Clara anyway. It's kinda nice being back on the ranch. You don't know how much a place means to you until you're away from it."

"Well, I'll try not to take up too much of your time. Shall we sit? I sent you both a series of questions I had about the operations up at Rabbit Creek. That was your brainchild, Martin, and now that you're up there with fresh eyes Stella, I thought maybe you might have some additional insights and fresh ideas to bring to the table."

"Sure. Sounds good." Stella nodded to Brandon, encouraging him to move forward with his questioning.

"Okay then. Martin, I'll start with you. Can you give me something of a history on using the federal land for grazing, and, to the degree you also use state or tribal lands? I would like to hear about that too." Brandon pulled a notebook and pen from his well-used canvas and leather back-pack and started making notes.

Martin provided history on the use of public lands and the wide variation in costs to the oper-ator. Without pausing, he turned to Stella and asked her to explain the benefits of controlled grazing on public lands. Brandon kept taking notes furiously as Stella spoke.

"Rising fuel and equipment prices hit ranchers hard. If you come watch the Rabbit Creek operation, you'll notice first and foremost that I'm running cattle in a rugged country where no equipment and vehicles can travel. I need a good horse and I rough it for days at a time. My team and I move cattle on horseback. We don't haul feed into the pastures. We provide minerals and salt, but we're not driving that all around the canyon."

"It makes sense that there would be a sub-stantial savings and cost avoidance using this model." Brandon looked from Stella to Martin, hoping one of them would volunteer the financial perspective. Stella obliged by sharing some rough figures.

"It goes beyond just the dollars and cents to me." Stella shifted in her chair and crossed her legs. She would soon share her passion for animal welfare.

"Can we be honest? I mean, if you look at big scale ranching and grow-feeder operations, like the one I grew up on, much of what the cattle endure goes against nature. They are fed food that puts weight on fast, burdening their bodies, and some ranchers expose their herd to hormones and chemicals that get passed on through their flesh. All that was standard practice, but now, consumers are demanding something else." Stella fought the urge to spring from her chair and start pacing and lecturing, with her arms waiving wildly as she tried to get her students to understand her perspective. Martin looked on with pride. Brandon paused his pen to acknowledge and reflect on her passion.

"Our customers are looking for fewer chemicals in their meat and more natural conditions for the livestock. As operators, we need to stand behind our product. These cattle that I'm running are eating off the land. They are grazing on cactus and shrubs and grasses. They have limited access to water. A subset of the population seeks them out because they are healthy, are not exposed to certain grains thought to be harmful for humans and their meat has a unique flavor, and it is lean."

"Thanks for bringing up the consumer's perspective. We hear more and more that the voice of the consumer carries increased weight in the marketplace." Brandon tapped the bottom of his pen against his legal pad as he contemplated his next question.

"All the talk of global warming, does that impact your operation?" Brandon looked to Martin. Martin looked to Stella, who was on the edge of her chair, poised to respond.

"It impacts our operation less than, shall we say, traditional operators? The cows on Rabbit Creek come from a long line of high desert animals. They are efficient and survive with limited water. The same is not true for those cattle eating grain and plentiful grass. They have to be watered regularly because they need it to help their bodies manage the high load of food and chemicals they process. If there is a decrease in water because of global warming, not only will the high desert cattle be better positioned to survive, but they are already accustomed to living on the scanty plants they eat. Cattle that are bred to stand in one place and eat green shoots will not tolerate drought."

Stella let Brandon catch up. He was writing feverishly.

"Sure, if there is a severe drought we may have to cut back the herd to prevent overgrazing of diminishing food. But that is minor compared to what will happen with the traditional rancher. They'll have to sell a whole herd or large portions because they'll run out of viable food sources. We have the added advantage that with frequent pasture rotation, to avoid overgrazing, our cattle are spreading plant seeds far and wide."

Martin smiled toward Stella. He wanted to stand and cheer. He hadn't even recognized this quality of his cattle in the context of drought recovery.

"Your passion is inspiring, Stella. You either have done a lot of homework or you're just brilliant at your job."

"Or both." Stella concluded.

"Would either of you like to comment on overhead costs?" Brandon drew a line on his notepad - a sign of transition to another topic.

"Stella's on a roll. Stella, go ahead, unless you want me to take this one."

"I'll start, you can finish if you have anything

else." Stella turned to Brandon. She wasn't sure that it was just her passion talking anymore. She felt a need to impress him. "If you think about it, the price of land is not cheap. Traditional ranchers look to increase their landholdings to increase their herd size. In our operation, our opportunity is to manage grazing. If we are careful with our observations, we know when to move cattle so the land can recover and we can graze the same section again. Care management of grazing is more affordable than buying more land. The increased availability of federal land at the current cow-calf unit price is a boon for our operation. I speculate that there is more grazing land available if we can show a value to the government."

Martin raised his eyebrows. It had been some years since he advocated for opening more grazing land. He and Stella would talk further about this idea.

"I don't live in a ranch-house because there is no need for a ranch at Rabbit Creek. The cattle are scattered in the canyons and forest. We are not harvesting or grinding feed so we don't need that equipment nor do we need to store it. We manage several smaller herds, rather than herds of large numbers, so we need less fencing and water. We also look at the natural resources differently from the traditional rancher. I'm measuring plant growth and environmental conditions that my dad never had to pay attention to, and he's a very successful rancher."

Stella sat back in her chair, satisfied that she had shared all her knowledge on the subject. Martin, Clara, and Brandon all looked at her, silent at first, then talking over each other, emphasizing various points that Stella made.

Brandon asked some clarifying questions and shared some anecdotes of operators attempting to implement innovative practices. "Well, unless you have something to add, Martin or Clara, I think I have all the information I can gather today and wow, is it great stuff!"

Brandon turned to Stella. "You know your stuff, Stella. This is great information and I promise, if I learn of anything that may be added value for you, I will share it."

"Thanks Brandon. I think Martin will agree that it's essential to inform oneself, and he has always encouraged me to challenge the status quo. In this industry we need to always ask what our customers want and need and find a way, within reason, to satisfy their demands."

"Well said, Stella." Martin nodded to Stella. "Brandon, if there's anything else you need, you know how to reach me."

The group rose as Brandon tucked his legal pad and pen back in his bag. He shook hands with Clara and Martin, thanking them for their time and hospitality, then turned to Stella. "Stella, do you mind walking me out?"

"I don't mind at all. I need to stretch my legs some." She walked toward the door with Brandon following close behind.

Brandon was silent, processing his thoughts on the way to his pickup. When he got to the driver's door, he turned to Stella. "You just blew my socks off. I mean, you've been at your job for what, a matter of weeks, and you've got this whole concept thought out."

"Well, I need be familiar with my job and it's more than herding cattle and fixing fences." Stella looked at Brandon, no smile crossing her lips.

"I'm sorry. I know you can do your job. It's just that what you just shared with me is a lot more thought out than I usually get. It helps that you're very articulate and can get your ideas across."

He paused and grinned. "Heck, have you ever thought of being a lawyer? You've got the skills."

"No, that's never even once crossed my mind! I'll leave that to you. I enjoy sleeping under the stars or running with a tarp over my head dodging rain drops while the cows look on trying to figure out what my problem is."

"It sounds like you're thrilled to be settled in Watson. I hope to come see you up there some day, if that's all right."

"Sure, why not? Well, Brandon..." Stella reached out and touched his bicep. "I think I've given you all I have today. I hope to see you again too, maybe after your Texas case is over? My mom and I got my house all in order. I could even cook you dinner, although I'm out of practice."

Brandon leaned in to close the gap between them. "That's okay. I'm heading off to Texas so you've got time to practice."

Stella reached out and opened Brandon's door for him. "That's good, I need it. I hope you find time to stay in touch. You just got an earful about my work. Next it will be your turn to share."

"There's a next time? Great! I look forward to it and yes, I should have something interesting to share by the next time I see you. For now, I've got to get to the office and type up my notes. The partners are waiting on this information. This is the last of the operator interviews and now I pack up about a dozen boxes of research and discovery, pack a suitcase and hit the road."

"You mean, you have to drive to Texas?"

"That's right. I need a vehicle down there and I have all this stuff to haul. That's why I won't be back for a while. I will stay in touch, though, if that's okay."

"I would like that. You take care of yourself down there."

"Me? I'll be fine. I have a room in a company condo about a mile from our office. It's not likely any wild animal will attack me. You, on the other hand, have a vast wilderness between you and your bed." Brandon reached to Stella's face and brushed her cheek with his finger. "You stay safe, beautiful."

She watched as he climbed into his pickup. They exchanged waves as he drove away. She turned toward the house to see Martin and Clara, arm in arm, watching from the porch.

"Now that was a sweet farewell!" Clara called out to Stella. "You'll be seeing that boy again, Stella. Mark my words."

15

—————

Stella settled into the routine of moving in and out of cow camp. She coordinated her activities, as best she could, with the weather forecast. She planned the two to five day overnight trail rides every other week or so. The moving parts kept her busy in-between, preparing food, packing and the most difficult, selecting the right clothes. Nights could be cold, and days in the sun very warm. She mastered the art of dressing in layers and became skilled at reducing or adding layers while riding.

Stella now carried an extra notebook with her. In the evenings she wrote down the thoughts that came to her during the ride. Much of what she wrote reflected the environment, her love for the cattle and the cowboy lifestyle she enjoyed.

Once in a while her lines rhymed or they would make her laugh when she read them later on the weekend.

Matt became Stella's main right-hand man when she needed help with the cattle or big fencing and hauling jobs. They often worked in silence for long periods during the day. If they were on an overnight job, they would share stories about childhood around the fire in the evening. Matt became animated when sharing stories about his children. Stella's heart melted to see him light up when he told about their newest milestone or antic.

Since she and Mom had furnished it and Gus moved in, Stella loved her new home. Gus proved to be every bit as good with the cattle as Jed bragged him up to be.

Martin drove up to Rabbit Creek Ranch about six weeks after their meeting at Winding Slough with Brandon. He delivered salt and mineral supplements and some back-up fencing materials.

"Looks like winter is coming up here. Bet it's chilly at night now, huh?" Martin pointed to the snow on top of the highest peaks in the distance.

"We haven't hit freezing yet, but I know it's coming before long. I picked up a new bedroll.

Cost about as much as my bed in the house but I'll be warm as a tick in fur in that sack."

"That's good. I'm glad you found something that'll work for you. I remember when Clara and I were first starting we stuffed potato sacks with straw or dried grass to put some insulation between us and the ground. A good tarp can be a lifesaver in the cold."

"I've got those too. Never can be too prepared."

"That's right. Well, if you don't need anything else, I guess I'll be heading back down south." Martin turned to return to his pickup. He shifted around to call out to Stella. "Say, did you ever hear anything more from Brandon after our interview? He sort of fell off the face of the earth. I haven't heard a word."

Stella had some brief text messages from him, just saying hello and letting her know he was still working in Texas. There were no follow-up questions after the interview. "No, not really. He just sent a message to say he's still working on their case in Fort Worth. Never said another thing about the operations after we met with you."

"Strange. Well, I hope it helps him somehow with his work. Say, you and I should get together and talk. The longer you're here the more ideas you'll have, I'm sure."

"That sounds good, Martin. My brother Jesse will be here in two weeks. I think he wants to stay with me for several weeks. I would like to bring him down to meet you. I might put him to work up here some. I've got a few big projects, and Matt will be with his family. They're going to Iowa to visit relatives."

"Sure, sure! Bring him on down. We would love to meet him and if he's half the worker you are I have no qualms with him filling in. You're doing a great job, Stella. Thanks for being here." Martin tipped his hat and climbed into the truck to drive back to Winding Slough. He left Stella feeling accomplished and appreciated. She knew she was fortunate. Not everyone had the open feedback from his or her boss that she enjoyed.

***

Stella thought a little about what Brandon's days might be like while working in Texas. She assumed he had meetings, interviews with clients and witnesses, gathered documents for discovery and did a lot of writing in the office. She was unfamiliar with the inner workings of a legal case or a law office and didn't feel one way or another about it. While driving into Watson for supplies, she thought about the long weeks Brandon had been away and wondered how he was handling the ongoing workload.

When she returned home, she checked on the horses, fed Gus and warmed up some left-over fish stew for herself. It was Friday evening and she had no plans. Stella pulled Brandon's number up on her phone and poised her thumb over the button to dial him. She put the phone down and got up to do the dishes. About an hour and a shot of whiskey later, she picked up the phone again and called Brandon. When there was no answer, she hung up. She didn't have a message to leave. She was lonely.

After tidying up the house and watering the plants her mother insisted she get to 'bring life into the place', Stella picked a movie and sat down to watch it with Gus at her feet. She woke up at midnight; the movie was over and her neck hurt from the awkward position of her head. Gus had crawled into his bed for the night. He raised his head as she stirred, but once reassured that all was right in the world, he went back to sleep. She checked her phone to see if Brandon sent a text message after her abandoned call. There were no messages. She stumbled to bed and slept restlessly the rest of the night.

Stella woke early the next morning. Unsettling dreams and a poor night's sleep left her irritated. Gus was happy to see her, his tail wagging as he stood by the door to outside. She knelt and scratched behind his ear, the way he loved.

Her phone had a single message. Her mother wished her a good weekend filled with relaxation and fun. Stella didn't respond. She made a cup of coffee and carried her laptop to the sofa. On a whim, she looked up the law firm Brandon worked for. Stella scrolled around the site and found Brandon's profile. They advertised him as a trial attorney representing farmers, ranchers and agricultural businesses against the government. Brandon's family had lived in Arizona for nearly two centuries; forging a farmer-rancher lifestyle that Brandon still took part in. There were many accolades listed from law school and a list of multiple task forces and special interest groups that he worked with. Stella pursed her lips and raised her eyebrows before closing the browser. It impressed her that at least his employer, if not industry leaders, saw the promise in young Brandon Cage. Stella leaned back against the sofa, put her feet up on the pine coffee table and finished her coffee.

She made another cup and dropped a piece of sourdough bread into the toaster. She pulled her muck boots on and stepped onto the back deck to look out at the horses. They were standing in the pasture, grazing. Molly walked up to the fence, about fifty feet away from Stella, who made a mental note to ride Molly over the weekend. Molly was not working as much as Ranger, and Stella missed spending time with her old friend. She decided it was time to pick up another horse, so no horse was left alone in the pasture. She had plenty of grazing land on this mini ranch. She must message Jesse. He was coming soon and could bring one out from the ranch if they were looking to retire one of their horses. Stella didn't need another workhorse, just a companion, mostly for Molly.

Stella sat at the new farmhouse table to eat her toast and drink more coffee. She opened the laptop again. Curiosity was getting the best of her this morning. She searched again for Brandon's law firm, but this time focused the search on Texas lawsuits in the news. It was an imprecise search that yielded pages of results, most of which had nothing to do Brandon. Buried on page seven was an article on a cattle industry website. The suit involved dozens of large cattle ranchers fighting against the meatpackers' monopoly. The photo heading the article showed the McGraw and Lipson legal team standing outside the courthouse. According to the article, they won a certain hearing, related to their case, which made a new law in Texas favoring the ranchers. Brandon was there and a beautiful, young blond woman stood beside him with her arm locked in his.

Stella closed the cover of the computer and walked back outside with Gus, leaving the coffee and toast untouched. She paced the length of the back porch three or four times, then walked to the garage to clean out the cab of her pickup. She didn't know what to make of the image. She had no standing to be jealous; but she was. She turned the radio on as she cleaned, attempting to drown out the debate in her head. Stella wanted to be Brandon's girl more than she knew. But seeing him entangled with the arms of another woman brought up that old default internal message. *"All men will abandon you!"* yelled from center stage.

An hour later, the cab of the pickup was more than clean. She called Gus into the house, grabbed the laptop and headed for town. Her inner angst needed an audience. Edna was all she had.

Maxine's was busy with the usual breakfast and coffee crowd. Edna was in the kitchen when Stella walked in. She took a booth in the corner and sat facing the wall, avoiding eye contact with the patrons. Edna came by with coffee in hand about five minutes later.

"Well, what have we here? You look like a stray that's been dumped by the side of the road." Edna slid into the seat across from Stella. "You need some Edna love, don't you? If you can hang around for a half hour, most of these folks will go away and I can sit with you. Until then, I'll make you a special breakfast. That all right with you?"

"Thanks Edna." As she rose to go back to work, Edna reached out to pat her friend's hands, folded on the laptop in front of her.

"Hey Edna…" Stella called after her friend. "You have WiFi here, right?"

Edna reached into her pocket and handed Stella a piece of paper with the WiFi address and password typed out. "Sure do. That's how I get the younger crowd to come in. They can use the WiFi as much as they want, but they have to order something besides water."

Edna returned a short time later with a side of bacon and a short stack of pancakes topped with homemade strawberry compote and a whipped cream happy face. Stella couldn't help but laugh at the gesture. Edna filled Stella's coffee cup and promised to return to chat as soon as she could.

Stella finished all the breakfast she could eat and set the plates aside. She scooted further into the booth and opened her laptop, connecting to Maxine's WiFi. She scrolled through her emails and started unsubscribing to the multitude of vendors that were now encouraging her to buy more furniture and home décor. Stella was done with furniture shopping, so she rid herself of this unwanted byproduct of online commerce.

Edna filled a coffee cup for herself and topped off Stella's. She took the breakfast dishes to the kitchen and returned to talk to Stella.

"So, what's caused this lost puppy dog look on this fine Saturday morning?" Stella took a sip of her coffee. "No, wait. Let me guess. I bet it has something to do with a certain handsome lawyer friend of yours. Have you heard from him? Did you figure out what that interview you did was all about?"

Stella slouched in her seat and tapped on her computer, pulling up the website she found with Brandon's picture on it. "No, I haven't heard from him. I dialed his number last night and then hung up when he didn't answer."

"You didn't leave a message? What's a guy supposed to think of that?"

"Don't know. Don't care."

"Okay. Something has set you off. Did Martin tell you something?"

"No. I saw Martin this week, and he hasn't heard a thing either. He's still stumped about that interview too. Brandon hasn't followed up with either of us."

"Well then, what is it that's got your pretty peacock feathers so ruffled?"

"Look at this, would ya?" Stella turned the computer around for Edna to see. She patiently waited for a reaction while Edna looked at the page. There was none. "Come on. How can you be so cool?'

"It looks like they had a win in their case. Isn't that a good thing?"

"Look closer. See that beautiful blonde in the dress? See how she's hanging all over Brandon?"

"Nope. All I see is a big group getting close for their picture with big smiles on their faces." Edna pushed the laptop back to Stella. "Stella, I don't think you've been honest with yourself about how you feel about this guy."

"That's what half my brain said after I saw this picture and felt so jealous."

"Yeah? And what did the other half of your brain say?"

"Every man will abandon you. That's the tape that plays in my head repeatedly."

"I can understand that after your experience with Hank, but you haven't even talked to Brandon to see what the story is. Also, you're the one who said, but didn't exactly say, that you're too busy for a relationship. Don't you think you're being a little unfair here?"

"It's possible. Sounds mostly like I need a therapist."

"Naw. You've got Edna to talk to." She smiled. "What do you want to do now?"

"I don't want to do anything except return to the bliss that was my life here in Watson before I saw that photo."

"You are making much more out of this than what it is. That's what I think. And another thing, you have way too much time on your hands when you're not working and it's making you irritable. Tell you what. I have someone covering for me tomorrow here at the diner. Jeff and I are heading out for a hike. He's promised a great lunch if I do the hike with him. You need to come along. I'm not taking 'no' for an answer."

"Thanks for the offer. Don't you need to

check with Jeff first? It would be good for me to get out and work off some of this irritability I'm feeling. This is so odd for me. I never let guys get me wound up like this."

"Honestly, you don't let guys in your life so how would you know?"

"So true." Stella looked into the eyes of her friend. "I'm so glad I met you."

"That's right. Best darn therapist you'll never have to pay for!"

They laughed. Edna pulled out her phone. "I'll let Jeff know you're coming. What he doesn't know is that I'm not much of a hiker. I can walk all day on this flat concrete floor here in the diner, but put me in the outdoors and I suddenly grow two left feet. It will be good to have you there to distract him from my incompetence."

16

Jesse's timing was perfect. A huge fire was raging in the national forest abutting the Rabbit Creek Ranch pasturelands. Stella needed the extra hand to push the cattle away from the forestland, across the river, and to new grazing pasture. It was about two weeks before ideal conditions for grazing in the new pasture, but under the circumstances the move was necessary.

This was Jesse's first visit to Rabbit Creek Ranch and his first exposure to high desert ranching. His brow furrowed as he studied the landscape passing by as they drove closer and closer to the canyons. "How on earth do you raise cattle out here? There's not enough grass to feed a momma and calf!"

Stella laughed. "I don't raise them. They raise themselves out there." She motioned across the pickup windshield toward the boulders, shrubs and dry grass. "They eat cactus and shrubs and survive on little water. I move them around so they can graze what grass there is and new plants and I drop off some supplements. They do all the rest on their own. Best calvers I've ever seen."

Stella's knowledge and confidence impressed her brother.

"That fool!" Stella slowed down to a crawl when she saw a red vehicle on the road near the entrance to the ranch land. As she moved closer, she recognized Brandon in the driver's seat of a new Cadillac Escalade. Already feeling the pressure of the fire and the intense work before her, unresolved feelings of jealousy and mistrust bubbled up.

Stella shouted an unwelcoming line at him. "Brandon Cage, as I live and breathe, out here getting dusty with the hired hands."

"Nice to see you, Stella. Looks like the fire's going to cause some damage up there. Hope you got all your cattle in." His piercing blue eyes held her fiery dark eyes steady.

Silently, she fumed. *"How dare he show up,*

Stella assured him they had the situation under control and she shooed him off to the city to rub elbows with pretty women and the rest of the suits that think they know what ranchers need. She was unkind to him, but she couldn't worry about that now. She needed to save the cattle. The possibility of the cattle panicking as the fire smoke moved into their territory worried Stella.

She felt Jesse looking at her, trying to figure out what just happened with Brandon. That was a story for another day or no day at all. "Let it rest, Jesse. We've got work to do."

Jesse obliged as they unloaded their supplies, packed and saddled the horses and headed out to rescue cattle.

THEY SPENT two nights with the cattle. Stella and Jesse were both restless and eager to get the cattle as far away from the raging fire as possible. The second night, as they sat around the campfire, Stella noticed Jesse studying the ridgelines on the horizon. As his attention turned to the fire, she told him stories of her days at Winding Slough Ranch. Many colorful characters came and went at Winding Slough. Clara and Martin were magnets for the unique, and they saw value in the unconventional. Not all the hands they attracted were well suited to the work of the ranch.

Stella told of a young cowboy who was sweet on her. Suddenly she was reciting a poem that had been dancing in her head for weeks. Rhyming stanzas rolled off her tongue as she told a partially true story of a drinking, snuff-chewing cowboy who worked briefly at the ranch. He was sweet on Stella, but she didn't give him the time of day. She focused on building her cowboy skills, so she had equal footing with any competent cowboy that came along.

Jesse was in awe of the fact that his sister wrote poetry. He wasn't as awed by the prose she told, but he had found a special kinship with her. "I write a little, too. I don't put a, what do you say, cadence, I guess, to it but I like to write."

"Awesome! I had no idea. Tell you what. There's a cowboy poet's gathering coming up." She got him to agree to go to the first night of the gathering, just to see what it was all about. Over the next week, they swapped stories and read some of each other's writings.

THE COWBOY POET'S gathering was entertaining. Jesse not only enjoyed the song-like style of some cowboys' recitations, but the lyrics themselves were entertaining. Some were serious and told stories of family history. Others were hysterical, and the poets had the crowd in tears. Halfway through the evening, Jesse leaned into Stella. "I think I've found my calling."

She gave him a thumbs-up and his grin lasted the entire next week.

JESSE MET a cowgirl artist at the event. Stella wrangled the two of them into a date the following weekend while she went to the ranch for a business meeting. Clara and Martin invited her to dinner with their accountant. They wanted to revisit their contingency plan. The recent fire prompted them to consider what would happen if the grazing land wasn't available or there were other threats to the herd. The invitation to participate in this high-level meeting boosted Stella's ego.

After dinner, the accountant excused herself. Martin asked Stella to stay. He had something to discuss with her. When he returned from walking the accountant to her car, Martin pulled a letter from his vest pocket. "You remember that meeting we had a few months ago with Brandon? We were right to question his motives."

Stella's eyes grew wide as she took the letter from Martin.

"Go ahead, read it. You'll be as shocked as I am."

The letter was written on stationery from an agricultural law association Stella had never heard of. "What is this association? Have you ever heard of them before?"

Clara responded. "I did some research on them. It looks like it's a group for lobbyists, attorneys and the high mucky-mucks in the agriculture industry associations. I had never heard of them before. Martin, you didn't know them either, right?"

"That's right. After I got this letter, I called Brandon. He told me about the association and gave me more information on this award. It's an annual thing they do, and it's the granddaddy of the awards for that show. Finish reading Stella." Martin nodded to Stella to continue reading.

Stella read the punch line out loud. "The Agriculture Law Association of America will recognize Winding Slough Ranch and the affiliated ranches operated by Martin and Clara Drake at the annual convention with the Excellence in Agriculture Award. Specifically, the innovation, animal health, and consumer voice aspects of your operation, based on the submission by Brandon Cage of the McGraw and Lipson law firm, will be highlighted during the presentation."

Stella's hands dropped to the table. She looked at Martin and Clara. "Congratulations! This says you will get the award next month at the big stock show in Colorado. That's amazing!"

She re-read parts of the letter. Her stomach churned.

"I called Brandon up right when I got this. It had me scratching my head. He apologized for being less than forthright when he met with us. Apparently their firm worked up six applications for consideration, and ours was the one they submitted to this organization. He couldn't tell us what he was doing in case they didn't choose us. I let Brandon know that we both felt a little uneasy after our meeting."

Stella turned pale. Clara reached out and rubbed her palm across Stella's shoulder. "Honey, are you all right? You look like you've seen a ghost."

"I'm fine. It's just that I wasn't very nice to Brandon. He showed up at Rabbit Creek last week, out of the blue, when Jesse and I were heading out to move the cattle away from the fire. This clandestine effort to get information for this big award, and some other stuff with Brandon has me unsettled. He must think I'm ungrateful."

"No, I don't think so." Martin returned to the table and poured them each more decaf. "I told him we can't go to the stock show to accept the award. We will help with the presentation materials he asked for and all that, but Clara's getting a new knee and we won't be able to travel."

"Oh, Clara! I didn't know."

"It's fine, dear. I should have done it two years ago, but I hate being laid up. We didn't know about this award when we scheduled surgery. And now that I have my nerve up, I will not cancel."

"That's right. I've seen people wait too long and suffer unnecessarily. My grandpa was like that and after the surgery and recovery he said he regretted waiting so long." Stella remembered her mom's dad living with them for the recovery period when she was in junior high. He was a sweet man who had since passed on.

"I asked Brandon if we could send a representative since there was no way we could go. He assured me that we can send whoever we want. When I suggested I would ask you, he lit up like a Christmas tree. He didn't seem to harbor any ill-will at all."

"That's a relief, but I will reach out to him and apologize. My stress got the best of me."

"Let it rest. It'll all work out." Clara never missed an opportunity to share her optimism. It had carried her through many a hardship in life.

"There's more." Martin and Clara had their heads together earlier, wanting to make this a big affair for their surrogate child.

"How can that be? This is already a big deal!"

"There are some incredible prizes that come with this award. There's a cash prize, an honorary seat on the board for that association, a trip and a pickup truck. I don't know how we never heard of this before except, we long ago stopped going to the stock shows. They don't really cater to our type of operation."

"That makes sense. You do specialize in desert cattle and all the stock shows I've been to focus on the Midwest, Plains and Texas ranchers."

"We will buy a table at the awards ceremony.

The money goes to scholarships for agricultural students and, as you might guess, that's near and dear to us." Clara nodded in agreement with her husband.

"First, I should ask, are you willing to go in our stead and accept the award?"

"It would be my pleasure." Stella squirmed in her seat like a child getting a sweet treat.

"Since we will have a table and you will be the only one there from Winding Slough, we think you should invite your family to join you. What do you think?" Martin looked at Stella eagerly, hoping she would accept their offer.

"That's a great idea! They go to the stock show sometimes, anyway. This would be a special occasion for Mom to get dolled up. That would thrill her to no end."

"Then it's settled. I have an assignment from Brandon to get some information together. You're working with that woman up there in Watson to put some marketing together for Rabbit Creek. Could she could put a rush on it so I can include that information say, in ten days?"

"I'm happy to ask Kendra if she can do that. Her business is fairly young so I'm thinking she would have the time." Stella did not share that Jesse was on a date with her as they spoke.

"That would be terrific. I'll leave it to you to reach out to your parents and then let me know if they will be there with you. Brandon may know some folks who would like to join the table. I'll let you know. I told him I would get back to him after I spoke with you. He may send you additional information about the event." Martin started stacking the dishes to clear the table. Stella rose to help.

"Leave the dishes, Stella. Martin and I will get them."

"Let me take this stack to the sink. It's the least I can do."

"Don't let me hold you up. You've got quite a drive yet to get back home." Clara was clearing the food from the table and dishing the leftovers into containers to take to the bunkhouse.

"I don't think I'll be driving. I will float home with all this good news you shared tonight. I am so proud and grateful to be working with you, who value all the right things. And now, you're being rewarded for doing what you know is right. Isn't it just amazing?"

"Stella, I do believe you are more excited than we are. We have always done the right thing because it's right. We never looked for outsiders to give us praise." Martin was filling the dishwasher as he spoke.

"That's what makes it even more special. We will highlight all these things you do right now so others can learn from you. It won't surprise me if you have traditional operators coming to visit so they can learn from you."

"That's possible. You know us. The door is always open." Clara smiled. "That means for you too, dear. You come visit us more often, okay?"

"I will do my best, Clara. You know how serious I am about my work."

"Yes, yes we do. We love you for that. It warms our heart to see you happy. We'll do what we can to help you stay that way."

"I will definitely come to visit when you are recovering from surgery and I'm guessing before this big show we will have to meet again. Martin, I know you'll be making notes of things you would say if you could go. Am I right?"

Martin grinned. "You know me well, Stella. You will do a fantastic job and yes, I may have some bullet points for you."

"I'm counting on it."

JESSE WAS SITTING at the kitchen table, writing.

She spilled all the news from the evening, including her history with Brandon.

"You've got some groveling to do, I think." Jesse reflected on his own relationship status and the missteps he may have taken.

"Sorry your evening wasn't more fun, Jesse. I guess it tells you what kind of girl you are not interested in, eh?"

"Kendra's beautiful and she's a lot of fun. I like my fun a little more intimate, I'd say." Jesse never was a party boy. He was more comfortable in smaller settings.

"I hope you will come with me to Colorado. You'll still be here next month, right?"

"I wouldn't miss this chance to see you on stage for anything! Besides, you might need my protection if that Brandon fellow isn't one to forgive easily." Jesse smiled.

"I think if I'm wearing the right dress, he will probably forgive me." Stella was researching the event online as they spoke. She looked at photos from prior years' award ceremonies to see what the customary attire was. Edna would know what she needed. Good thing she had invited Jeff and Edna out for Sunday dinner.

"Oh, no!" Stella closed her laptop abruptly and looked at Jesse.

"What's the matter?"

"I almost forgot! We're hosting dinner tomorrow for Edna and Jeff. I have no idea what I'm serving."

Jesse laughed. "There's the old faithful Yvette Davies kitchen sink lasagna. I think together we can figure that one out, throw a salad together, butter some French bread and open a bottle of wine."

"You're the best, brother!"

"Yeah, we've got this."

17

Stella felt like a schoolgirl getting ready for prom. She packed a curling iron and makeup in an overnight bag with jeans and t-shirts. She and Edna spent a day in the city finding a dress and the assorted essentials to go with it. The makeup she packed probably wouldn't see the light of day again after the Stock Show activities. Edna had her convinced that the spotlights would make her look sickly without makeup, so she caved in.

The dress they found was classy. After trying on two dozen dresses in varying styles and shades of black, Edna brought a cobalt blue dress to the dressing room. Stella was grateful for some color. The dress was fitted with capped sleeves and it fell just below her knees, accentuating her toned calves. They found some midnight blue strappy shoes and a beaded handbag to finish the look.

Before leaving the shopping center, Edna nudged Stella into one last shop. "I think you should take a back-up outfit just in case there is another fancy event after hours. Sometimes that happens, there's an after-party or a special dinner to go to."

Stella shrugged and followed Edna into yet another store. They passed by racks of short cocktail dresses. Stella was too modest to wear those dresses. In the back of the store, they found racks of holiday-colored satins.

"These wide legs are popular, aren't they?" Stella held out a pair of black satin pants with hems as wide as the waist. "I need a boot cut."

Edna laughed as she searched through the rack.

"I've got it!" Edna held out black satin pants fitted at the ankle, a silver sleeveless blouse, and wide satin tie with a rhinestone buckle.

"Now that, I like." Stella tried it on, paid for it and they headed home.

EVERYTHING WAS PACKED into Jesse's truck for the trip to Colorado. Jesse was satisfied to wear a new pair of blue jeans and his only dress jacket, which their mother was bringing from Buffalo Ridge.

Sitting behind the steering wheel, Jesse looked at his sister. "Do you have all your clothes and makeup?"

"Check."

"All your props and your speech?"

"I can't believe it. Hang on." Stella jumped out of the pickup and ran into the house. Gus wasn't there to greet her. Matt took Gus to his house for the few days that Stella would be gone. She was paying him to check on the horses and the house, too.

Stella hopped back into the truck with laptop and charger in hand. "I can't believe I almost forgot this. I'm still working on my acceptance speech. Martin keeps sending me things he would like me to mention if there's time."

"This is will make a good story one day, I can feel it in my bones." Everything was becoming something to write about for Jesse. The more he wrote, the better he got and the more he found to say.

The trip to Denver was about twelve hours of driving time. With a stop for lunch, they would be there by mid-evening. Their parents would arrive the following day. They drove through Utah and just across the border into Colorado before they grabbed fast food for lunch. There were few options before that.

"We're making great time. Thanks for doing the driving." Stella looked up from her computer. She had read and revised her notes a dozen times so far on the journey.

"You're welcome. This gives you time to polish your speech. You're such a perfectionist."

Stella reached over and nudged Jesse's arm with her fist. "Takes one to know one."

"Just look at who raised us. They set the bar high." Jesse always felt pressure to live up to what he thought his parents' expectations were. Being the last of four children, a lot of successes preceded him. He wrote about family and western life frequently.

The trip to Denver was uneventful. They checked into their hotel rooms. The association provided Stella's room; the Drakes paid for Jesse's. When the desk clerk said she had a suite in the swanky hotel, Stella didn't know what to say. They rode the elevator in silence, managing their own luggage. Stella and Jesse were both tired from the long drive and thought they were ready for bed. Jesse got off on the sixteenth floor.

They agreed to meet for breakfast at seven the next morning.

Stella got off on the thirty-second floor and found room 3216. She opened the door, and the sweet smell of flowers greeted her. There were a dozen bouquets in the room and two baskets of fruit, wine, cheese, and chocolates. She hung up her garment bag, dropped the other bags on the floor and grabbed her phone.

"Jesse, you've got to come up here and see this." She spouted as she looked out the massive windows at the city lights below. "Room 3216. No, wait! I have to come to get you. Your key won't let you up past the thirtieth floor. I'll be right down."

Stella raced out the door to the elevator. Jesse was waiting for her at the elevator, standing in stocking feet, shirt untucked. "What's the big deal? So, you got a nice room."

"Yeah. You'll see how nice. Come on." She tugged his arm and pulled him into the elevator.

"Holy smoke! Where did all this stuff come from? Are you sure you have the right room?" The massive bouquets and baskets were impressive.

"Here, let's have a midnight snack. Cheese and crackers? White wine or red?" The two picked at the baskets, snacking and reading the cards on the gifts.

"I don't even know who some of these people are. I get the association, the law firm, Brandon, Martin and Clara, even Mom and Dad. The rest of these, I don't know who they came from."

Jesse took the stack of cards from Stella and looked through them. "I can't help you, sis. It's a mystery to me. But when you find out where they came from, tell them I enjoyed the food and drink."

Stella walked into the bar and kitchen area of the suite. She opened the refrigerator to peer inside, thinking it would be empty. There was a box of pastries, a plate of desserts, more fruit and an assortment of beer. She grabbed the envelope taped to the refrigerator door and tore it open. The gifts in the fridge were from the production company in charge of the event. They invited her to join them the following morning to get familiar with the room where the award ceremony would take place, the stage, and the sound system. She handed the note to Jesse. "These people think I'm here to work."

"Did you think this was just going to be one big party? You have to work for it!" Jesse drank the last bit of wine from his glass. "I'm heading to bed. It's been a long day. Shall we still meet for breakfast?"

"Yes. But can we make it for eight? I might have a little trouble winding down tonight."

"Works for me. See you then."

Stella bounced around the room, smelling the flowers, putting cheese and champagne in the refrigerator and studying the gift cards once again. She pulled out her computer and re-searched the names she wasn't familiar with. Some of them were prior years' recipients. She wrote an email to Martin and Clara, detailing the gifts and sent pictures so they could share in the fun.

Stella's phone chimed just as she was ready to crawl into bed. *I hope you made it to the hotel and your room is acceptable. I have a delay and won't get in until right before the ceremony tomorrow night. Can we catch up after?*

Stella was surprised that Brandon, or anyone from his firm, had not asked to review her speech or review the program. Brandon had sent a few texts checking in and making basic in-quiries, like the names of her family that would join her at the event. Martin had shared the ma-terials he sent. Brandon incorporated it into the media presentation assembled for an introduc-tion to the Winding Slough Ranch operation.

Martin and Clara videoed an acceptance message and introduced Stella since they couldn't be there.

She quickly typed a return message. *I hope this all comes together. I'm a little, no, a lot out of my element here.*

STELLA HAD the best night's sleep she'd had in several weeks. She woke fifteen minutes before eight. She pulled her hair back, threw on jeans and a western shirt and headed to the lobby to meet Jesse for breakfast. She found him talking to some men in suits.

"Here she is now. Gentlemen, this is my sister, Stella Davies." The men introduced themselves as being from the sponsoring association. They were from different parts of the country and gathered early in the morning for a business meeting.

"Congratulations, Stella! The application Brandon submitted about your operation thoroughly impressed us. I realize the Drakes are the owners but I have to tell you, I had a teleconference with them after the association decided to give them the award and they sang your praises. This really is an outstanding organization and what you're doing up there on Rabbit Creek should be a lesson for many."

The knowledge that these men had about the Drakes, their operation…and her…took Stella by surprise. "Thank you, sir. Thanks to all of you. It really is an honor to be here to represent the Winding Slough operations. Martin and Clara have a vision like no other I have encountered, and I was raised on a ranch in South Dakota."

"That's right. You're from the Davies family on Buffalo Ridge. Hi, I'm Buck Cordas. I come from the Fort Piere area. I met your dad and two of your brothers some time ago. Steve, and Chance, I think. Chance, he's the pro bull rider, right?"

"That's right. My parents and brother Steve, along with Jesse here, will be at the ceremony tonight. A little moral support, you might say. It really is a pleasure to meet all of you and to be accepting your award tonight. I promise I won't show up like this, in my jeans." The group laughed.

"It would be fine if you did. The story tonight will carry the show. I'm sure you'll have a lot of color to add, whether you're wearing jeans or something else." Weston Moore, a board member from Texas, shook Stella's hand. "We need to meet the rest of our group and get this meeting started. Remember, after this Winding Slough will have a representative at our board meetings."

Stella waved them all off. She bumped up against Jesse. "So bro, how about that breakfast?"

"Is that how you're going to play this? You're all famous and everything and all you can do is talk about breakfast? Okay, I'm in."

The restaurant served a huge European breakfast with an omelet bar on the side. There was something available for everyone. Stella and Jesse ate two and three plates of food, trying a little of everything and more of the things they liked.

"Who needs a special box of pastries and big baskets of chocolate and cheese when you can come down here and eat fish balls and pickled herring? This place is the bomb!"

STELLA AND JESSE met with Kerry from the production company in the banquet hall. Kerry walked through the motions of getting on and off stage and using the sound system. They programmed the media presentation to play on the big screen behind her and smaller screens throughout the room.

"So, everyone in the room will have a close-up view of this mug." Stella joked with the production manager.

"That's right, and aren't they the lucky ones?" He smiled back at Stella and they continued their walk-through. Jesse watched from their designated table directly in front of center-stage.

After the walk-through, Jesse and Stella explored the hotel and nearby shops. They were in a swanky part of town, so window-shopping was more than enough to satisfy their curiosity. Their mom, dad, and brother Steve arrived in time to meet for lunch. As always, it was a happy reunion for the family. The group hung out in Stella's suite after lunch. The view and the motherlode of gifts bestowed on Stella equally awed Yvette and Dan.

Dan put his arm around his daughter. "How does it feel to be a celebrity?"

"It feels like a lot of pressure. I hope I can pull off the presentation tonight."

"Oh Stella, you are such a worrier! You take after your mother."

"I don't get my worrying from the dirt." She tapped her elbow into Dan's ribs. The group laughed. Dan worried with the best of them. He worried silently, but they all knew when he was concerned for his family, his crops or his cattle. He paced, checked and re-checked the animals and fields, and started coffee drinking extra early during stressful times. "I've seen you worry a time or two yourself."

Stella rehearsed her acceptance speech and presentation of the Winding Slough Ranch conglomerate for them.

"Oh my, you are giving me goose bumps Stella. I feel like I missed some of your growing up. You're such a polished speaker. You will have them spellbound tonight." Yvette sniffed and wiped the corners of her eyes. A proud momma moment!

"I have to agree with your mother. You are a fantastic presenter. That whole audience will pay attention. First, you're just so beautiful, and second, your passion for the ranch shines through. Even if your words weren't eloquent, which they are, your passion alone could carry you through. Terrific job, honey." Dan was nervous for his daughter but believed strongly that she would give a stellar performance, just like when she was barrel racing or running track. She was a performer. "Jesse, what do you think?"

"First off, I've heard this speech for hours at

a time in the truck, so the message is familiar. I would say Stella did a great job crafting it. Second, she's always running off reciting some poem or another so I know she has the stage presence to deliver." Jesse winked at his sister and grinned.

"All right, you guys, that's enough! Anyone want something from the drink and snack baskets before we get ready? The banquet starts at 6:00 with announcements, some association business, then dinner and finally, the awards."

"I think we should have a little toast before we break up this little party." Yvette turned to Dan and asked him to open a bottle of champagne from the refrigerator. She dug her phone out to take some photos.

"A little bubbly would be good about now." Stella felt jumpy as she thought about walking around in high heels and a dress with make-up and curls in her hair. "Mom, will you guys come back up here so we can all go together? I might need help with my dress."

"Sure. I think that's a great idea. You need chaperones to shield you from the paparazzi. Okay now, everyone squeeze in so I can get a big selfie to send back home. Raise your glasses, but not in front of your face. On the count of three everyone say 'bubbles' and hold your smile. Ready? One. Two. Three. Bubbles!"

Yvette snapped their photo a few times. They clanked their glasses, downed the champagne and dispersed to their respective rooms to get ready. Stella checked the time. It was four thirty-seven. She had time for a bath before getting dressed.

For fifteen minutes she soaked in the tub, listening to her favorite country-western music and thinking about her high desert cows. She missed them.

18

———

The Davies family walked with the mass of people into the dining hall that seated over five hundred guests. Yvette slipped her hand into the crook of Stella's arm. "Isn't this lovely? Everything looks so elegant."

"Yes, it's gorgeous." Stella held her breath. *Breathe, Stella, breathe.*

Stella saw Brandon out of the corner of her eye. He was watching the crowd file in through the ballroom doors. When he saw Stella, he gasped quietly, then stepped forward and offered her his hand. "Stella! You look stunning!"

"Hello, Brandon. It's great to see you." Stella instinctively brushed her free hand down her hip to make sure her dress wasn't riding up.

"Won't you and your chaperones please

come this way? I would like to introduce you to the firm partners."

She turned to her family. "Let's go over here with Brandon."

Brandon made introductions, and the group exchanged handshakes. It surprised Stella that he remembered her family's names and where they were from. He even knew which brother was which.

"Can we chat for just a minute?" Brandon pulled Stella aside, his arm around her shoulders.

"Why don't you guys go to our table. Jesse knows where it is. I'll be there in a minute or two." Stella turned to Brandon, who steered her to a corner, away from the busy entrance.

"Brandon, I... I owe you..." Stella put her hand on Brandon's forearm, wanting to clear the air before the night began.

"Stella, please. Don't worry about any of that now. We can talk about it later. I just wanted a moment alone with you, to soak in your radiance. I'll tell you all about stuff later but I must tell you this now. I've been a fool to not pursue you. I can't get you out of my mind, even though I haven't been in touch. Anyway, how are you feeling about tonight? Are you feeling good? You sure look fantastic. The audience may not even notice what you're saying because you're so beautiful."

"Brandon! I hope that's not true." Stella looked down and stuck out her lower lip in a feigned pout. "I've worked hard on my speech. My family gave me high marks when I was rehearsing this afternoon."

She smiled up at him and got lost in his blue eyes.

"I'm sure it will be brilliant. I won't keep you any longer. You have your family here to spend time with. But we're still on for tonight, right? I'm inviting your family to a reception in the firm's suite. After that I really need to talk with you. Does that still work for you?"

"Yes. I look forward to it."

"Wonderful. Now..." Brandon leaned in and kissed Stella's cheek. "Good luck and I'll see you on stage."

"Thanks, Brandon." She squeezed his hand, smiled, and turned as gracefully as she could in high heels.

***

"So, that's Brandon." Yvette didn't let Stella sit before she started talking. "He is such a gentleman and, oh my, he's handsome."

Jesse hadn't taken his eyes off his sister. He knew she was as anxious about seeing Brandon tonight as she was about her presentation, if not more so. Concern showed on his face as he studied his sister. "You okay?"

Stella smiled at Jesse. "Perfect, thank you."

She was. Her anxiety diminished almost entirely. She told jokes and pointed out fashion faux pas to her mom in quiet side talk. "I don't mean to be ugly, but I mean, some things just ask to be made fun of."

"Stella, be nice and hope that your seams don't split while you're on stage!"

Stella tapped her mother's arm. "Mom, now you've jinxed me! Okay, I'll be good."

Several attendees at neighboring tables introduced themselves. The law firm partners and association board members who Stella met previously brought their spouses to the Davies table for introductions. Stella was distracted. She felt only an occasional twinge of a nervous belly.

The evening program was entertaining, and dinner was superb. As desserts were being distributed, the association president, David Coombs, took the stage and introduced Brandon.

"With me here on stage is Mr. Brandon Cage. Brandon comes to us from the Phoenix branch of McGraw and Lipson, a firm known to most of us as a leader in pursuing the rights of agriculture operators. Brandon submitted the dossier for the winning nominee of tonight's Excellence in Agriculture Award. Brandon, I believe you've put together a presentation for us and have a representative of the winner to introduce." The audience welcomed Brandon with applause.

"Thank you, David. That's right, I have a presentation for you and I believe you will find, as our firm and the association did, this is a very deserving recipient. Before the presentation, I invite Stella Davies to the stage."

Stella navigated her way to the stage while Brandon continued to speak. 'Stella manages one of the ranches for the award winners. I've seen this woman in action and I can tell you, you want to stay out of her way when she's working cattle. She is more cowboy than many cowboys I've met. Please welcome Stella Davies."

The audience clapped as she paused at the bottom of the stage stairs while the production crew fitted her with a wireless microphone before joining Brandon on stage.

"Thank you, Brandon and thank you to all you lovely people in the audience for the warm welcome."

She looked to the Davies table to make sure Yvette was recording the presentation for the Drakes. Reassured that she was, Stella smiled at her mom and nodded.

"Stella, thank you for joining me up here. I know you have some things to share with the audience later, but I invited you up here during this part of the presentation so you can elaborate on my comments or correct me if I run afoul. Sound good?"

Stella nodded, feeling at ease on the stage. "Sounds great Brandon. You've done your homework so I don't think there will be any corrections."

She looked from Brandon to the audience. "He put the owners and I through a grueling interview, without telling us what it was for. You can imagine the shock when we learned we won this award."

She looked back at Brandon. "I still haven't forgiven you for that, you know."

Brandon laughed with the audience. "Well folks, it looks like I have some amends to make. Let's see if I adequately put into words and pictures the story of Winding Slough Ranch, which is not only a single ranch but a collection of multiple ranches owned by Martin and Clara Drake of northern Arizona."

Brandon designed the media presentation with perfection. Martin and Clara were humble and sincere in their videotaped introduction and acceptance. Brandon incorporated aerial and ground photos of all the ranches, the hands working and driving cattle, the thriving crops and the varied landscape.

"Now these next photos will be a surprise to you, Stella. I don't think you've seen them before." Brandon displayed a series of aerial photos taken the first day of Stella and Jesse's efforts to relocate the cattle away from the fire. The images were intense as they first showed the immense fire in the neighboring forest, and then transitioned to images of Jesse and Stella herding the cattle from canyons and behind boulders to the well-worn trail they followed to safer grazing lands. Jesse and Stella's expression of determination could only be seen in their eyes. The rest of their faces were hidden behind wet bandanas to filter the smoky air.

At the end of that segment, there were evening photos of Jesse and Stella around the campfire. The audience clapped to see western life alive and well.

"You're right, Brandon, I had not seen those pictures. In fact, I didn't even know you had a drone out there. We'll have a talk about this later too. Meanwhile, I would like to introduce my brother Jesse Davies who was with me on that ride." Stella pointed to Jesse. "Jesse stand up and wave to all these nice people."

Jesse obliged and smiled. The audience responded with applause.

"How did I do, Stella, did I get the details correct?" Brandon turned to his stage mate.

"I would give you an A-plus Brandon." She turned to the audience. "Let's give Brandon a great big hand for pulling all this information together and making such a fabulous media presentation." The audience delivered enthusiastic applause.

"I'm going to turn the stage over to you now, Stella. I know you have some more personal things to share and more details about the innovative way you are approaching the high desert herding experience. I suspect Martin asked you to share a few things on his behalf as well." Brandon winked at Stella. "Once again, here is Stella Davies of the Winding Slough Ranch operations."

"Thank you all again for that kind reception." Stella reached for a stack of paper from the podium. "You're right Brandon, Martin is a thinking man, and he loves to stay in touch with me."

She held up the stack of paper. They were index cards, taped together accordion fashion to make a long chain of cards when unfurled. "Here are just some of the messages he sent me to share with you all."

Stella held the top card above her head and let the stack of taped cards unfold to make a long chain that reached the floor. The audience laughed.

Over the next twenty minutes, Stella shared more history of the ranch, her journey from a green cowboy to a foreman on the most challenging and interesting ranch in the operation. Her impassioned pleas to ranchers and operators to evaluate their practices and find ways to improve animal health and conserve resources moved the audience. Some scratched notes on cocktail napkins, some took pictures of the images displayed on screen, and others sat listening intently and nodded. Her efforts were rewarded with a standing ovation.

19

———

*B*randon escorted Stella off the stage at the conclusion of her presentation. A reception line spontaneously developed around them as they fielded questions. Stella handed out Winding Slough business cards to those who asked, and there were many. Newly formed fans overtook the Davies family table. They fielded all the questions they could about Stella and the ranch, and answered questions about their own operation. Many recognized the Davies name from the rodeo circuit and Chance's professional bull riding fame.

Later, Stella and her family joined Brandon at the post-event gathering in the law firm's extra-large suite. Stella had become a star that night. The firm partners loved her and praised her for her impassioned presentation. They invited her to join their firm as a per diem speaker. She promised to consider the invitation.

Dan and Yvette left for their hotel room about an hour into the party. "It's been a long day for us. We'll see you for breakfast, Stella. Brandon, it was a real pleasure to meet you."

Dan hugged his daughter, and shook Brandon's hand before escorting Yvette out of the room. About thirty minutes later, Jesse and Steve invited Stella and Brandon to join them in the lounge for a nightcap. They politely declined. Stella agreed to see them in the morning. "Bring a doggie bag, Steve, the breakfast is impressive."

"Well, Stella, you are truly the belle of the ball." Brandon leaned in and kissed her cheek. He whispered in her ear. "You blew their socks off! Mine too."

Stella stepped back. "Thank you. Now, let's talk about those photos, shall we?"

Brandon's brow furrowed as he looked at her stern face, which quickly melted into a smile. "That was pretty gutsy of you to fly a drone with the forest service planes up there checking conditions."

"I had to do it, Stella. There was no better time to capture you in action. You were so fired up and on a mission. I have to say though, I don't think you were very nice to me that day." Brandon looked at her, the corners of his mouth drooped, creases formed in his forehead and he looked away. He looked back and smiled as Stella started her explanation.

"You are right. I'm sorry. I wasn't very nice. There's no excuse. But I learned a lot about myself around that time."

"Anything you care to share? Wait. Let's find someplace less...noisy and crowded, shall we?"

"Sure. Why don't you come to my suite? I can show you all the wonderful gifts I got. I can make some coffee, or there's plenty of alcohol and soda up there if you prefer."

THEY CONTINUED their conversation in chairs facing the night skyline view from Stella's suite. "Okay, where were we? Oh yes, you were going to tell me about some self-discovery."

Stella looked around and grabbed her phone. She pulled up the picture of Brandon and the beautiful woman that had set her off so badly those many weeks before. "I was setting up house, getting established in my home and fighting the urge to text you every ten minutes. I was trying to convince myself that someday, it would be nice to have you in my life. The truth is, I wanted you in my life then. Anyway, I didn't hear anything from you when you were in Texas."

Stella paused and took a sip of coffee. She wanted to be fully present for this conversation.

"Something came over me. I was almost obsessing, I think. I started looking online to see if I could learn anything about the case you were working on. Low and behold, this picture popped up." She showed the picture to Brandon.

"That was a big day. That ruling changed the entire complexion of the case. In fact, because of that ruling we were able to mediate the case this week. That's why I couldn't come until later today. I had to pack all the documents and bring them with me. I'm going from here back to Arizona for the foreseeable future. Anyway, I guess I don't understand what you're saying about that picture."

"Well, I saw that beautiful woman with her arm in yours and I got jealous."

A loud laugh burst out from Brandon, nearly spraying coffee onto the window. "Jealous? Oh, Stella! There's nothing to be jealous of. That beautiful woman is Mrs. Julia Sands. She works for our firm in the Texas office. She's very friendly like that, but she's very married and I would never think of her as a woman to pursue. Sorry you had that experience."

He reached out and gently stroked Stella's face.

"It was then that I realized how much I care for you Brandon and how much my heart wants to be with you. So when I saw you at Rabbit Creek Ranch, I was all wound up. I was worried about the cattle, it was Jesse's first time out in the high desert with me and he wasn't familiar with the ranch, and then there you come in a shiny new... whatever you were driving… with a shit-eating grin on your face. I lost it."

Brandon stood up and scooted his chair closer to Stella. He took her hand in his. She felt a flare of excitement as their fingers interlaced. "I accept your apology. I understand. I thought about you working around men all the time, even though I know you're too professional to even think about seeing one of them. We all have weak moments. When we won that motion, I started talking with the partners about the like-lihood that we would settle that case and I wouldn't need to spend many more months in Texas. I talked to them about the possibility of changing the structure of my work. I need some-where where I can be closer to you. Spending time with you is all I think about Stella, a lot of the time. I just know that you and I are a great pair. I mean, look at us up there on stage tonight. It was like dancing with you, and we didn't miss a beat. Stella, I'm crazy about you and I want to be with you."

He studied Stella's face for a reaction.

She looked at him and the tears pooling in her eyes ran down her cheeks. "Can you really make that happen? Can we be close enough to actually spend time together and see if what we are feeling is what we think it is?"

"You mean is it the real deal? Is it love? The kind that our parents have? The kind that Martin and Clara have?"

"Yes, that's what I need to know. I feel it in here." Stella put her hand on her chest. "But I want to know in here." She pointed to her head.

"It's enough for me to know that you feel it in your heart, Stella. I do too. Yes, I worked something out with the firm so I can work remotely, with good Internet connectivity, three weeks every month. I may have to travel to client meetings during that time, but I will not be away for weeks or months at a time anymore. I'll spend time at my parents' ranch and you and I can figure out how we will spend time together while we're exploring us."

Stella pulled Brandon's face close to hers. She kissed him on the cheek.

"One of the partners pulled me aside tonight and said I would be crazy not to pursue you. They were serious when they offered you a speaking position with them. You were amazing and with more women in agriculture, it would be fantastic to have you as a spokesperson."

"I'll think about it. I think, though, that I will be busy exploring other opportunities. Brandon, you have made me a very happy cowboy."

Brandon laughed. "It will be a hoot telling people my girlfriend is a cowboy. You're breaking new trail Stella, and I will be there to witness as you do. I love you, Stella Davies."

ACKNOWLEDGMENTS

Many thanks to those who helped make this book possible including the amazing Linda Zeppa - author, coach, intuitive and creative, cover designer, Deborah, of Tugboat Designs and proofreader Angela. You have been an amazing group to work with!

ABOUT THE AUTHOR

Kim Smart was raised on the edge of the Badlands in western South Dakota, but *grew up* in
Alaska after landing there as a young nurse. Two
decades later, she moved to San Diego to attend
law school. After graduating, she returned to
Alaska to again work in health care, this time at
the intersection with law and public service.

Kim has always had a diverse love for writing
and reading, enjoying romance, women's literature, historical fiction, poetry, and stories of
people living authentic lives. Following a lifelong
dream, Kim has turned to writing. She currently
writes romance, women's literature, and historical fiction, along with nonfiction articles for various publications.

When not writing or traveling, Kim enjoys time
with her parents and extended family, hiking and
creating in the kitchen. She presently lives in Arizona, or wherever the wind blows her as she

visits her children, grandchildren, and other interesting parts of our world. She has much to write about and many stories to tell!

Join Kim to learn about new releases and exclusive reader giveaways at: https://kimsmartauthor.com

BUFFALO RIDGE RANCH SERIES

Falling for Home - Book 1

Jesse Davies had been in love with his hometown girl for as long as he could remember. As they drift apart, he searches for meaning in his life. To find love, he must first find his voice and find himself.

Kerry Braun had dreams larger than Buffalo Ridge. To pursue her dreams, she leaves everything behind. The pursuit to become a veterinarian consumes her, blocking out all opportunities for lasting love. Will she ever find her way back?

Can two small-town friends find happily-ever-after?

The first novel in Kim Smart's Buffalo Ridge Ranch series tugs at emotions as the dance of love tests the boundaries of happily-ever-after.

Two for Love - Book 2

Steve Davies lived his life in the shadow of his late

wife's dreams. To emerge from his grief, he must take a chance. Hoping to expand the dreams they had together, he starts a dude ranch. In the process, he hires a cook - a city girl who brings along her son.

Bella Giordano needed to find safety for her young son. On a whim, she moves them from Manhattan to the Badlands of South Dakota, hoping the small town life, away from mob threats and smog, will be good for them both.

Will grief dissolve and a new opportunity be enough to build a new family?

The second novel in Kim Smart's Buffalo Ridge Ranch series sets the table for new opportunities and the possibility of love. Will hurts heal and love grow?

Taking Chances - BOOK 3

Chance Davies, champion bull rider, goes from being rock star of the rodeo to broken and lost after a final ride turns into a tragic accident. He is forced to return to Buffalo Ridge Ranch for recuperation after many years on the circuit. Through hard work and challenging himself, his body starts to heal. But will he allow his mind and spirit to heal and open up to new opportunities?

Sheltered from love, Pauline Whyte was always a

misfit in the small town of Buffalo Ridge where everyone knew her family's business. She escaped the town gossip for a few years by moving away, only to have to return to care for her ailing father. Somehow, in this small town, love finds its way to her. Can she accept it?

To let love in, they must overcome loss and pain. Will her misfit ways fit into his new life for a happily-ever-after?

The third novel in Kim Smart's Buffalo Ridge Ranch series brings a story of overcoming the odds. Is that enough to find true love?

STANDALONE NOVELS

Tangled Ribbons

The essences of individual humans are substantially more alike than they are different. Gertie Hall lives this truth as she rises from the young child of a Hitler's henchman to a world-renown advocate for human rights. Through scientific endeavors, humanitarian efforts and a tireless fight to right the wrongs of her father, she explores her feminine self, intellect, ingenuity, and grit.

A hole remains in her soul where two childhood friends were ripped away, and Gertie's own father was complicit in the disappearance of their families. *Tangled Ribbons*, scene by scene, captures the life of Gertie, intertwined with the stories of her friends, Sarah and Hannah, who flee fiery Berlin and establish new identities and new lives in far away places. Late in their lives, Gertie offers a heart-wrenching plea for amends and a new generation is enfolded in their healing.

Christmas Market Reunion

Brooke Linton, 26, is stuck in a rut, aggressively pursuing professional recognition in corporate Miami with little time for fun. She tries to convince herself that life is great, so long as she has a good job, family at Christmas and she can sing in the church choir.

A chance meeting with an American in Amsterdam gives Brooke a glimpse into what life could be like outside the office.

After returning from vacation, her professional world falls apart. Through soul searching and discussion with a sister, Brooke grows to see this as an opening to create a life of her dreams. Little did she know how far those dreams would take her.

This sweet, wholesome romance will surprise and delight you with world travel, unexpected encounters, and fairytale weddings. The question remains. Can a chance encounter on foreign soil turn into something more? Get Christmas Market Reunion today and lose yourself in happily ever after.